My House of Dreams

Susan Kite

To Jordan
God bless you and
Happy reading !
Susan
Kite

2012

BookLocker.com, Inc.
2010

To: Fr. Ben Innes, who introduced me to the wonders of the Mission San Luis Rey. To Susan Schuck, Ellen Richie and so many others for not allowing this story to die. To my husband, Dan for his unwavering support. And to my dear, dear friend, Patricia Crumpler, who has worked many hours editing, listening and encouraging. Thank you so much.

Chapter One

Mission San Luis Obispo, spring, 1798.

Father Antonio Peyri bent over a sturdy plank table in the dappled shade of a large oak and examined the drawings he had sketched the previous month. Pieces of broken adobe held down each corner so the paper would stay flat as he study it. A beetle crawled across one of his sandals and he shook it off. Dust coated the cuffs of his gray woolen habit and he shook that off, too. He tightened the cincture around his slim waist, hearing the reassuring click of the prayer beads and cross that dangled from the end.

Soft salt-tinged breeze from the ocean cooled his sweaty brow and he returned to the design. With a sharpened piece of charcoal Antonio made a slight change in the drawing of the statue that would be placed above the doorway of the new building. He felt urgency; he wanted to get this building finished before the full heat of the summer arrived.

Workers had just formed the adobe bricks used to construct the walls, and in his mind's eye Antonio could already picture how the completed building would look. His intense blue eyes searched for more changes. This time he could find none. It was a house for the increasing neophyte (Indian convert) population, but he also wanted it to be pleasant to look at and last for many years.

Antonio heard footsteps and stood up straighter when he saw not only the head of San Luis Obispo, Father Miguel Giribet, but also the head missionary of this part of New Spain, Father Presidente Fermin de Lasuén. The young priest had no idea why the President of the California mission system had come here. Even Father Giribet expressed surprise when Father de Lasuén appeared with his retinue the day before yesterday. Since that time the Father Presidente had either been in conference with Father Miguel or touring the mission grounds.

Without a word, the Father Presidente studied Antonio's drawings. He glanced at the small trenches neophytes were digging for the footings of the new building. "Father Miguel, last year the number of neophytes joining the mission was a third again what it was the year before?"

"Yes, Father Presidente," Father Miguel said.

"And there has been an increase in the herds?"

"Yes."

"You have sent glowing reports of this young missionary, who puts so much of himself in his designs for new buildings and in the teaching of the neophytes," Father Presidente said.

"Yes, Father Presidente. He does indeed."

Father Presidente turned to Antonio, who was embarrassed by the attention. "My son, we are not saying these things to boast. These are facts. Your work has been exemplary since your arrival in Alta California."

Antonio bowed his head. "I am here to serve, Father Presidente. That is why I joined the order."

"I know, Father Antonio," de Lasuén said. "You have served well. You came to this mission when?"

"Two years ago, Father," Antonio wondered why the Father Presidente asked. Surely he would already know that.

The old cleric took a deep breath. "Father Antonio Peyri, based on the reports of Father Giribet and what I have seen with my own eyes, it is the will of God that I appoint you head missionary of the new mission to be built between San Juan Capistrano and San Diego."

Antonio fell to his knees, head bowed, crossing himself. "To God goes all service and glory. Praise be to His Holy Name."

Payomkawichum lands, Spring, 1798

An eagle flew high above shimmering waves of heat. Below a young Payomkawichum, alone near the northern boundaries of his people's territory noted the passage of the great bird as a favorable omen and returned his scrutiny to the task before him. Noki closed his eyes and intoned a quick invocation to the gods as he prepared to chip at the small piece of chert he held firmly over a large flat stone. His brows furrowed in concentration and he licked his lips before making the first strike on what he hoped would become a perfect arrowhead. This was a slow process, one that took much practice. Noki's time practicing was evidenced by the littering of small flakes of chert, flint and quartzite that lay scattered around the flat chipping block. This time, Noki, who would be twelve years old at the time of the next new moon, was determined to craft a perfect arrow point that would make Father proud. Noki's father, Kwalah, was the chief weapon maker and Noki dreamed of someday being declared worthy to follow in his father's footsteps.

Noki had already mastered the choosing of the right woods for spear handles and the carving of bullroarers. He had begun making practice bows for the younger boys, but arrow points had thus far eluded him. He gazed at the small stone in his fingers, willing it to reveal the place where the right piece of rock would flake off. He ignored the rustlings of small creatures near his feet, insects buzzing around his ears, the heat of the sun on his bare back. Noki's eyes were focused on the grayish stone before him.

He continued studying the seams and cracks in the jagged stone, waiting for it to open up its soul to his soul, to allow him to see into its very heart. He picked up one of his tools, a cutting stone. It was flat on top and narrow at the bottom. Noki didn't look at it as he examined the piece of chert. Sweat trickled down his face, around the corner of his mouth and dripped from his chin. Finally, with his left hand Noki laid the narrow point of his tool against the place on the stone he felt was the fracture point. With his eyes focused on the chert and the pointed stone above it, he picked up another stone, one he would use to make the deciding blow. Taking in a slow breath he brought his right hand down, hitting the top of the cutting tool with just the force needed.

The stone fractured cleanly and two perfect halves lay on the flat block Noki was using as his worktable. He studied the two pieces, finding them both suitable for use as arrowheads. "Thank you, Brother Eagle," he breathed, his eyes flicking up at the dark shape still circling overhead. He was confident that Father would be pleased. If he made good arrowheads with chert, Noki was sure Father would allow him to use obsidian, the most prized stone of all. A young man of eleven winters could not wish for any greater honor. Pulling back a strand of hair that had fallen in his face and tucking it behind his ear, Noki studied the two almost perfect arrowheads. He needed to remove a few more flakes of stone from one and then both arrowheads would be perfectly balanced. He held the arrowhead steady as he tapped it with the deer-antler pilaxpish, the tool he used to do the more delicate work. Tiny flakes fell away until Noki was satisfied. Wrapping the finished arrowheads in small pieces of rabbit fur, he placed them in the pouch he had made for this purpose.

Noki picked up another stone. This one had the look and feel of a spearhead, but he studied it as he had the previous one. He laid the chipping tool against the place he felt was best to get a clean fracture. He raised the striking tool.

"Noki!" a child's voice broke into his concentration. "Noki!" He forced his irritation away. It was Eti, his little brother. Noki could never stay angry with Eti. At seven winters, his brother was the same height as a child of six. Eti was his father's oldest child by his present wife, Tahmahwit. Noki's own mother, Shehevish, had died the winter he was four years old. While Noki could vaguely remember her, it was Tahmahwit whom he called Mother.

Ever the worrier and always curious, Eti brought Noki every bit of gossip and every scrap of news that reached his ears. His brother stared at him with large, dark eyes filled with worry. Noki swiped his hand across his forehead, trying to push aside strands of hair that had again escaped from the leather tieback. The strands flopped back in his face.

"Th . . . th . . . they come, N . . . Noki!" Eti stuttered. Noki figured his brother was anxious about something. Eti seldom stuttered when they were together.

"Who?" Noki asked. "Who comes?"

"Who?" Eti repeated, taking a deep breath when he saw Noki signing for him to calm down. "Wh . . . where have you been, Noki? For days the old ones have been t . . . talking about the s . . . s. . . . strangers."

The strangers.... Noki wasn't that worried about them. Still, he had heard about the strangers living close to the ocean "The old ones fret too much. The white strangers came a few years ago and left after a few days," he reassured Eti as he put his chert and flint samples in a leather pouch at his side. He put the chipping tools into a different pouch. It would do no good to try and make more arrowheads now. His concentration was gone.

Noki straightened up, stretching away the kinks in his legs. "I suppose you would like to see these strangers for yourself," he teased.

Eti's eyes widened. "Y . . . yes!"

"If they come close enough to the village this time, we can spy on them. Maybe Father will want to trade with them and he will take us with him," Noki said. Father's arrowheads and spear points were prized among the tribes in the region and he was always welcome in their villages. Noki wondered if the white strangers would be as eager. "Let's go home." He picked up his own weapons; a stone knife and a spear. Noki made the knife himself. He had chipped the edge of the dark stone, fastened the finished stone into the notched top of the bone, holding it in place with deer sinew that had been soaked in the stream. When he had tied the sinew in place and it was dry, the handle and stone seemed to be a single piece.

Noki had also made the spear, but under the close tutelage of his father. It was balanced perfectly for him and with the wakut, his throwing stick, had the potential to bring down a fully-grown deer. As he picked his way down the hill, he watched for more stones to make arrow points. Noki picked up several and added them to his pouch.

"Come on, Noki," Eti called. "It's getting late!"

Noki climbed down quickly, though he wasn't as sure-footed as his brother.

Outside of the village, the two boys stopped at a stream flowing through the meadow. Before taking a drink of the cold, clear water, Noki looked skyward again and saw the eagle still floating above him, catching the winds that blew in from the ocean.

"Come on. Let's race!" Noki challenged.

Eti grinned at him. "You must have made good arrowheads today."

"Yes!" Unable to wait, Noki pulled out one of the new arrow points, unwrapping it from its protective fur covering. The perfectly shaped arrowhead sat in Noki's cupped hand.

Eti peered at it, but refrained from touching the arrowhead. To touch it before the weapon master examined it might be enough to render the weapon useless or make the gods angry.

"Ah, Father will like this," Eti said, his voice filled with awe at his brother's accomplishment.

"I hope so," Noki replied. His father was talented and patient. Noki's first remembrances were Father's strong fingers around his little pudgy ones, showing him how to hold the chipping stone.

Father never ridiculed his mistakes, but he expected Noki to do his best. An arrowhead that was almost perfect would not hit the rabbit a family needed for its dinner. So far, all of the arrowheads Noki had made would not hit any rabbits. *Hopefully*, thought Noki, *that will change today.* He re-wrapped the arrowhead and put it back in the pouch. He repeated his challenge. "Let's race!"

Eti laughed and dashed toward the village, his feet as nimble as an antelope's. With a grin, Noki grabbed his weapons and leaped after him, but did not catch up to Eti until they reached the sweat lodge on the outskirts of the village. In the short races, no one could equal Eti. In the long races, Noki had the ability to pass his brother and win, but he almost never did. He felt the hard earth under his tough bare soles and the cooling breeze that blew in his face as he ran.

He leaped across the stream and ran alongside Eti, his pouches thumping against his side. Ahpaho, one of the younger mothers in the village, looked up from where she was pounding tule reeds and greeted them as they flew by. The boys called back to her as they continued racing into the village. They ran past cone-shaped homes, slowing as they approached the large ceremonial house. They stopped when they saw the shaman inside the fence that surrounded part of the ceremonial house. The boys peered between the loose fitted willow branch posts, watching Kawawish sprinkle sand of various colors in a pattern only the shaman knew. The old man intoned a chant invoking the spirits to strike some unseen enemy.

Noki pulled Eti's arm and drew him away. It was bad luck to look upon the shaman as he worked. Kawawish's chant followed them as they walked to their house.

Noki watched the women setting baskets out and he knew it was time for the food gathering expedition to the ocean. Fresh fish would be a welcome change. Noki hoped they would find a beached whale. Once before that had happened and he remembered the fat layered slabs of meat roasting over open fires. They had eaten well that season.

Tahmahwit greeted them. She, too, was laying out baskets, filling them with dried sweet grasses and sage to take away any stale odors. His little sister rested in her cradleboard leaning against their house, her dark eyes watching everything around her.

"Are we g . . . g . . . going to the beach?" Eti jumped up and down, like his namesake the squirrel, his eyes gleaming in anticipation.

"Yes, Eti, we are going in two days. This morning, our men came back with permission from the other tribes to cross their lands," she replied. "There is much to do and both of you will have to help prepare."

Noki was well aware of the work involved in moving the tribe from one location to another. Each of the seasons brought carefully planned trips to different areas, such as the beach, or the mountain oak groves for acorns. It was a pattern that varied little from year to year.

The work involved could not dampen Eti's anticipation of playing on the beach. Any trip was an adventure to him. Noki felt the same way, although he knew, because he was almost a man, he would be expected to do more work this year. If Father liked his arrowheads, perhaps he would be allowed to trade them for better materials, like obsidian.

Touching one of the hide bags resting against his thigh, Noki said, "What would you like us to do, Mother?"

She looked into his eyes and smiled. Tahmahwit could tell he had had a good day in the hills. She could always tell. She used the mother's arts to feel into his soul. Noki's aunt, Sachac, had once told him Shehevish had left a part of her own heart in Tahmahwit so she could raise him.

"You will help your father mend the tools he'll need for the hunts on the water. Eti, you will help me collect the baskets and fix the nets."

Eti stepped to her side eager to help, as though his speed with these chores would make the beginning of the adventure come sooner. Noki was more interested in Father's judgment of his arrowheads. He left to find his father, who was probably in the sweathouse.

The sweathouse was built of long poles covered with a thick, even layer of mud plaster. A large deer hide covered the doorway. The building lay over a foundation dug a foot below the surface of the ground.

Because he had not passed his manhood rituals yet, Noki was not allowed inside. He waited several paces outside the doorway. Squatting down, he began drawing designs in the dust. Noki drew pictures of arrowheads, perfect ones set on straight, strong sticks, feathered for exact balance on the other end. He continued to sketch his desire, making the arrow fly straight, killing a huge buck.

A foot shoved his hand aside and rubbed out the drawing. "A grubby fingered little stone chipper cannot presume to make the powerful magic!" a low voice growled.

Indignant at the insult, Noki had a ready retort on his lips, but realized it was Kawawish, the shaman. He remembered that within a half year he would be going through the manhood ceremonies. A man did not give in to impetuous speech or actions. Noki tempered his voice, "Yes, Honored One."

The shaman's eyes showed their disdain, but for an instant the look changed to something Noki couldn't decipher. *Fear?* Then Kawawish disappeared into the sweathouse.

Chapter Two

Noki noticed his balled fists and willed himself to relax. He watched the dust settle near his feet. The past week Kawawish had been acting as though he was chewing on bumblebees. Noki was just drawing for fun. At least he thought that was all he was doing. Maybe it *was* taboo. Still, the reprimand had been more like an insult. Noki looked for the eagle that had been watching over him, but it was gone. There were only shimmering waves of heat.

The leather flap rustled and he saw his father come out of the sweathouse, his body freshly scraped clean of sweat and dust. Restraining the impulse to immediately show his father his arrowheads, he got up with what he hoped was a dignified demeanor. "What would you like me to do to prepare for our journey to the ocean?"

"Several things, but first you must remember to let the shaman make the holy drawings."

Noki dug his toe into the offending dust.

"Come with me," Kwalah said, his voice showing no displeasure. They strode out of the village on a path Noki knew well. It led to the small canyon that had been used as a quarry for several generations. Kwalah walked up a narrow trail and stopped at a shallow cave. "Noki, sit down. I have never told you how Kawawish came to our village."

"I thought he had always lived here."

"No, he came from a place several days southeast of here. He was a young man at the time, but old enough to have a wife and a baby son."

Noki was puzzled. Kawawish and his wife had no children that he knew of. "There is no son here now."

"That's because the son died before Kawawish came here," Kwalah replied.

"What happened?"

"Kawawish was preparing to become the shaman of his village, learning under an old man loved by the people. He married the captain's daughter and they were blessed with a son. One night he had a dream of terrible animals coming to eat the people up. It was so vivid that he went into the mountains to pray and fast.

"What did the gods tell him?"

"I don't know, but after many days, he went back home and found his village destroyed. His house had been torn down and a blood-stained bone-rattle lay in the fire pit."

"What happened to all the people?"

"Kawawish traveled to the next village, but found that sickness had killed many of the people there. One of the elders told him of white-skinned men from the south that had come riding on strange beasts. One of the white men wore a shiny vest and hat. He tried to take some of the young women and men from Kawawish's village. The men fought back, and the strangers killed most of them, using weapons that made thunderous noise. In the captain's house lay Kawawish's wife, beaten cruelly, unable to raise her head to greet her husband. Their baby was dead."

Noki had wondered at her stooped back and scarred face. Now he understood. "Why would anyone kill a baby?"

"Perhaps someone whose heart was stone, Noki. Kawawish followed the tracks of the invaders to take his revenge on them, but after a while the gods whispered for him to use his magic against them instead. I want you to remember this story, but do not let it make your heart sad, only more understanding. Let us have faith in the gods." Kwalah glanced back into the cave. "You will be helping me gather stones for fishing spears. I also want you to help me make fishhooks."

Fishhooks were usually made from deer antlers and it took more patience to carve them. Up until now, Noki had only been able to practice on unusable fragments of deer antler. Now Father was trusting him with the more difficult task of making the barbed hooks. Deciding this was the right time to show Father his arrowheads, he reached into his pouch. "I have something to show you, Father," he said as he pulled out his treasures.

"Ah, I wondered what had you so eager to find me," Kwalah replied. "You've been gone much the past moon cycle. Is this the reason?"

"Yes!" Noki handed his father the arrowheads, giving him the best one last. He waited while Father examined them; feeling them with his thumb and holding them close to his face to examine the edges. He let each one rest on his palm to test the balance. After the examination, Kwalah laid each arrowhead back on the rabbit skin Noki had spread out on the floor of the cave.

Kwalah closed his fingers over the last stone point. "You have every right to be eager, Noki. These are fine arrowheads, especially this one." He handed the last stone to Noki, who wrapped them all in the skin before putting them back into his pouch.

"I think you should keep those to barter with the other tribes we meet at the ocean. They will bring you much in trade," Kwalah added.

"Thank you, Father," Noki replied, pleased.

"It's your right, my son," he said, laying his hand on Noki's arm. "Now, let's find something we can work on this evening. There's not much daylight left."

Noki began chipping at the rock wall of the little cave, watching as the pieces fell to the ground. Sometimes he stopped to examine more promising stones, putting usable ones in his father's large pouch. Kwalah did the same.

For several minutes they worked side by side without saying anything. "Where did you find the rocks for your arrowheads? You didn't find them here," Kwalah asked.

"There's a hillside to the southeast of the village. I've been working there for the last seven days."

"We'll have to look at it together when we return from the ocean. You found excellent stones there."

Noki flushed with pleasure. His father never bestowed empty praise They searched, dug and gathered for another hour. Noki noted the bulging pouch at his father's side. There would be many good fishing and hunting spears for this trip.

"We'll begin shaping these stones at first light tomorrow. Lamqaat has been selecting the straight wood for the shafts." They gathered up their tools and headed back home. The setting sun bathed the landscape in burnished gold. Soon the gold changed to soft black velvet, but the pair walked the path to the village with the ease of those who knew every tiny part of their small universe.

Fires snapped and crackled, many with meat roasting on spits over their flames. Everyone greeted Father and Noki cheerfully as they passed. As they approached their own house, Noki smelled dinner. Mother was making rabbit soup from Eti's kill earlier in the day. Eti had an unerring eye with a wakut, the throwing stick, and at close range, was developing the same expertise with a bow.

Noki couldn't resist. He leaned over and tried to stick his finger in the soup for a taste. Tahmahwit pushed his hand away and threw in a pinch of salt. His stomach growled its displeasure.

Little Atu, Noki's sister watched them from her cradleboard. Her eyes sparkled in merriment when she saw him. Noki tickled Atu's pudgy chin and she laughed and clapped her hands. Atu looked at her hand in surprise, amazed at this new thing she had accomplished. She clapped again and looked up to see who was watching. Noki clapped his hands with her.

"Supper is almost ready," Tahmahwit said with a soft laugh. "Tell your impatient stomach to wait a little while longer."

"I will, Mother." Noki replied and slipped into the mat covered house. His father was examining the stones they had collected as he sat by a glowing fire in the middle of their home. He motioned to Noki to sit by him. The dimness of the room didn't deter Kwalah. The most gifted weapon makers were able to feel the soul of their stones. Noki had felt some of that today.

Father pushed the pile of rocks in front of his son. "You did well today. I want you to examine these rocks we gathered. Hear what the spirits tell you about them. Choose those you feel will make good, strong spearheads."

Noki looked up in surprise. Him choose? Again, his father was showing him honor. He studied the rocks in front of him. Most were chert or quartz, excellent for making spears. Noki laid the stones out in a row and shifted his body so the firelight could play on all of the choices. He took a deep breath and bent close to study the stones.

In the dim light, Noki could see that several would not be good enough to work with. Young boys' practice spears, perhaps, but not the big spears needed for heavy prey like seals. He set those stones aside and resisted the temptation to look into his father's face. Noki picked up the rest of the rocks one at a time, asking for the gods' help. He felt promise in some and nothing in others. When he was finished, there were fifteen stones lying in front of Kwalah. Now he looked up at his father, feeling curiously drained.

Father gathered the chosen stones and put them in his pouch. "We will make the spearheads tomorrow."

Noki could not believe his ears. "Aren't you going to check them?"

"No. The proof of your choosing will come tomorrow morning."

Tahmahwit was spooning out the savory soup with a carved wooden ladle into pottery bowls. She also handed them pieces of acorn flour flatbread. Noki savored the meal, spooning out small chunks of meat and eating them before drinking the delicious broth. Mother had to be the best cook in the village, he thought as he gave his full stomach a pat.

Tacayme, late Spring, 1798

Father Presidente Fermín de Lasuén led a large procession from San Juan Capistrano, with Fathers Antonio Peyri and Juan Norberto de Santiago by his side. Behind them were several foot soldiers and a young officer on horseback. A dozen neophytes and their families followed. There were three cargo wagons, their huge wooden wheels groaning loudly as sturdy mules pulled them down the dusty highway. The wagons were loaded with many supplies needed for the beginnings of a new mission, including blankets and cloth, pickaxes, seed and plows. There were also the materials needed to celebrate Mass and teach the Indians; the robes, the Missal, chalices, the Christus, Holy Oil, an altar, a simple baptismal font, bells, and rosaries. Once the High Mass was held to establish the Mission San Luis Rey de Francia, cattle, goats, sheep and more seed would be sent from the two nearby missions in San Diego and San Juan Capistrano.

Antonio had spent much of the past two months on his knees or consulting with Father de Lasuén. He had literally worn out a habit. It amazed him that he had been in the new world for just two years and now he was heading a new mission! Sometimes he wondered if God was playing a cruel joke on him.

They had walked since early morning, stopping for the mid-day meal and a short siesta during the hottest time of the afternoon. Antonio glanced sideways at the Father Presidente. The old cleric showed amazing energy and strength for someone of his advance years.

"Soon we will be coming to the trail that leads to the site of the new mission," the Father Presidente said as they walked.

Antonio noticed that the three missionaries' staffs were marking a unified time against the ground as they walked, matching the softer patter of their sandals. Unity in their walk, their purpose, their mission for God.

"Ah, Father Antonio, the valley…. It is perfect," Father de Lasuén announced.

Antonio had heard this same thing before, not only from the Father Presidente, but also from others who had been in these rolling hills. He couldn't wait to see it. He wished he had been able to come earlier, right after his calling, but he would be there soon enough.

The Father Presidente began reminiscing again. "I came here last year, in the fall." Father de Lasuén's voice took on an almost dreamy quality. The staffs continued to thump in time on the hard-packed earth as he spoke. "This place was explored almost thirty years ago, and was called San Juan

Capistrano el Viejo." He chuckled. "It was a source of confusion when the Mission San Juan Capistrano was established seven years later. But as there was nothing important about Old Capistrano, as this area began to be called, it was of no consequence."

"But now it will have a new name," Father Juan Norberto de Santiago interjected.

The Father Presidente continued, "Yes, a grand name for a grand and holy place. There is a small river, fed with streams from the hills. As the mission grows, that might be a problem in dryer years, but nothing insurmountable. But the meadows and hills! They are beautiful. There are many Indian villages, some right within the confines of the valley itself. Many neophytes in the Mission San Diego are from this area. I feel good things about this place."

Antonio did, too. He had read the accounts and was eager to begin his work here.

"My heart tells me that you will do a work that will continue long after I am dead, Antonio," the older priest said, as though knowing what he was thinking.

"With the help and grace of God."

"Indeed." Father de Lasuén stopped abruptly and stared around him. The whole procession halted and waited.

"Reverend Father," the soldier on horseback called out. "I believe that is the trail leading to Old Capistrano." He pointed southwest.

"Yes, it is, my son," Father President replied. The new trail was narrower and a harder for the wagons to negotiate, but they continued at a steady pace until they crested a hill and looked upon a broad valley. Rolling hills grew higher in the east. Antonio knew this was the place for the new mission. This was Old Capistrano, or in the language of the natives, Tacayme.

Antonio gazed upon the valley, struck by its beauty. Near a small river tules waved in the late afternoon breeze, while here and there an old willow hung drooping branches over the water. In the distance, smoke drifted skyward, evidence of native rancherias, or villages. He looked in all directions and counted three rancherias, one close to a league distant. The harvest would be great in this place, Antonio thought.

"We will camp down near the river and begin building tomorrow," Father de Lasuén declared.

"Father Presidente," a voice broke in. It was Ygnacio, an older neophyte from Mission San Juan Capistrano. He was the leader of the group of Indians accompanying them.

17

"Yes, my son?"

"The elders of the nearest village will come to visit tomorrow," Ygnacio said. "Perhaps they will not like it that others live on their land."

The Father Presidente looked thoughtful. "I don't think we have much to worry about. Once they are part of the Holy Mother Church, they will be happy we are here."

"It is so, Father Presidente," Ygnacio agreed. "But sometimes, in anger, a captain will act before thinking. I will say prayers that they are friendly."

Antonio was familiar with the designation of 'captain;' it was like an alcalde or mayor.

"Thank you, Ygnacio," Father de Lasuén said. "It would be a good idea for us all to pray for success. If need be, God forbid, we do have the soldiers."

"That is so, Father Presidente," Ygnacio intoned.

As the soldiers and neophytes set up camp, Antonio waded across the river and up one of the eastern hills. He stood at the top and watched the sun slide below the horizon. The hillside was bathed in a golden glow that made him think of the avenues of heaven. A breeze cooled his face and brought scents of pine and juniper. Several doves called to each other and a solitary bat darted above him catching insects.

Antonio remembered the first Mass he had celebrated, barely five years ago. That had been in Spain. He remembered the exhilaration of the moment, which had been the culmination of his ordination to the Holy Priesthood. Shortly after that he had been called to the New World. When he set sail, the trip had been quick, the winds furious and his stomach had threatened to retreat back to Cadiz. He had spent a short time at the college in Mexico and then traveled to San Luis Obispo.

Antonio took off his hat, looked toward the sun as it sank beyond the far hills and began to sing, "You are God; we praise you, You are the Lord; we acclaim you; You are the eternal Father; All creation worships you....." Antonio closed his eyes and sang the rest of the Te Deum. His mellow baritone voice continued, strengthening and becoming louder. When he finished, it seemed that everything had ceased its singing to listen.

"That was most appropriate, my son," the Father Presidente said. Antonio was startled, not having noticed him approach. "Could you begin again and we can sing it together?"

Antonio nodded and began the song once more. Father de Lasuén's deeper voice blended perfectly with his and they sang all three verses.

They watched the twilight deepen into soft velvet blackness. Stars appeared, winking brightly. "I think there is some dinner ready for us," the Father Presidente said after they had meditated for a while.

After prayers and dinner, Antonio lay down but found it difficult to go to sleep. He listened to the various creatures of the river peeping, croaking and chirping. He found it to be a soothing symphony and he fell asleep dreaming of the future.

Chapter Three

As the dawn painted the sky above the eastern hills, a bell roused those still asleep. Antonio had been awake for more than an hour. It had been too dark to walk and meditate as he usually did first thing in the morning, but he hadn't needed light to see where things were in this beautiful valley. Yesterday, it had been imprinted on his memory. He walked this valley in his mind. He felt the chill waters at the edge of the river and recounted the steps to the top of the hill. His imagination constructed the buildings, cultivated the fields and orchards, and filled the chapel with believers. Just before Father Juan rang the bell, Antonio prayed for the ability to make what was in his mind a reality.

After Mass everyone worked to build a temporary chapel. The Father Presidente walked down to the small river and paced out the distance from it to the spot where he determined a permanent church would eventually stand. It was exactly where Antonio had envisioned it. "The men's house should be over there," Antonio said, taking a stick to mark the spot he had selected. "The women's house here. There is a perfect piece of land for an orchard." He continued pointing out and marking the corners for various buildings. Forgotten for a moment was the man walking beside him. He remembered and flushed in embarrassment.

"Antonio, this is your mission. Continue."

"Fathers," a voice interrupted. It was Ygnacio and he was pointing toward one of the wagons.

A half a league beyond their camp, near a thicket, Antonio saw four Indians sitting on the ground. They were naked except for two wearing tule reed cloaks woven with feathers. Antonio marveled at their ability to approach the camp without being seen before now.

The soldiers snatched up their weapons.

"No, stay back," Father de Lasuén ordered them. He motioned to Antonio. "Come, let's greet our visitors."

The Indians rose from the ground in a single fluid motion. The Father Presidente greeted them with a smile and open hands. One of the cloaked men said something unintelligible. Antonio glanced at Ygnacio for translation.

"I don't know all the words, Father."

"Do the best you can, Ygnacio.

"They want us to leave."

Antonio considered that for a moment. "Who are the men in cloaks?"

"One is the captain, the leader of the village. The other with the eagle claw necklace is the shaman."

"Ygnacio, get four blankets out of the wagon and one of the necklaces, one with a Cristos on it. Get out a bolt of colorful material, if we have any, and one of the smaller iron pots," Antonio instructed.

"Yes, Father."

As the neophyte hastened to do his bidding, Antonio bowed to the Indian captain and signed that they had gifts for them. When Ygnacio returned, the Father Presidente presented the gifts to the captain. The Indian leader felt the blankets and took the one that appealed to him. When Father de Lasuén held up the necklaces, the captain's eyes widened and stared at the tiny figure of Christ dangling at the bottom.

Antonio tried to explain what the small carving represented. Finally, the captain said a word in his language and put the beads around his neck, holding the tiny Cristos in his hand and pointing to the sky. Antonio and Father de Lasuén said 'yes' at the same time. The shaman studied the crucifix and spoke.

Ygnacio translated. "The shaman says our god is tiny. Not a good god."

Antonio had no answer to that, but asked the Indian leader if they would like to come to their camp later to learn more about Christ and share food with them. He didn't know what to expect, but was pleased when the captain signed that they would come during the early afternoon. Without further word, the four Indians walked back toward their village.

"You are very capable with hand signs," Father de Lasuén said, his face showing pleasure at this turn of events. "The soldiers and some of the neophytes must go hunting so we can have an adequate dinner for our guests."

As the tribe made its way toward the sea, Noki felt a sense of tired satisfaction. For two days he and Father had shaped stones and tied them on the shafts. His fingers had blisters and his back ached, but all of his stones had been usable. Kwalah declared his weapons good to the hunters who came to barter. He displayed Noki's spears, arrowheads, and declared him worthy of being his successor.

Noki pulled a travois containing their trade items. Eti helped Mother carry extra baskets she had made for gathering fish and mussels. When he wasn't laden, Eti skipped along, singing songs of his own making, his words tumbling over each other at times.

Noki understood his brother's excitement. He couldn't help feeling this would be a very lucrative trip now that he was allowed to barter things he made. The tribes living near the ocean had interesting things to barter, like shells, carved whalebone knives and spoons, combs and ornaments.

"I hear you have much to trade this year," a familiar voice called. It was Koowut, his best friend. Slightly taller, though younger by several moon cycles; Koowut was ungainly, his feet having grown much faster than the rest of him. He was one of the few people Noki's age who had not made fun of Eti. Noki felt a closeness toward Koowut that he didn't feel for any of the other boys in the village. "Yes, Father has given me great honor," Noki said.

"Ha! You were worried," Koowut teased. "I wasn't."

Noki grinned and the two of them bantered until Koowut fell back to join his own family.

They walked all day, stopping at midday to eat and rest. When they started out again, Kawawish and the elders took them on a different route, one more south than the one they normally took through Quechla valley. Puzzled, Noki asked his father.

"Because of the Sosabitom," Father replied.

After hearing Kawawish's story, Noki was fearful of these white people. Still, he was curious and wanted to get a glimpse of them.

The tribe set up camp in a narrow valley not too far from the Quechla Valley. Noki gathered his bow, arrows and throwing stick and announced, "It would be good to have fresh meat for our dinner. I'm going hunting."

Kwalah was reclining against a boulder, his weapon making tools within easy reach. "Both of you?" he asked.

Eti was standing next to him, his own bow and arrows in his hands.

"I was planning on hunting alone," Noki replied.

"We'll go together," Father said. "I want to observe the Sosabitom, too. The elders will be meeting tonight to discuss the white men. Go on. I'll join you shortly."

When they were out of the camp, Eti grabbed Noki's arm. "You didn't want me t . . .to come with you."

Noki had wanted to be the first to spy on the Sosabitom, but he hadn't wanted to hurt Eti's feelings. "I'm sorry, Eti." The hurt look faded from his brother's face. "Remember though, you have to stay close and do what Father and I say." Noki headed in the direction of the white man's camp. Eti padded silently behind him. They watched for wood rats and rabbits, but saw nothing before their father joined them.

Long before they reached the white man's camp, wood smoke told them where the strangers were. The Sosabitom had camped on the banks of a small river. A small village of the people lay nearby. The white men wore clothes that covered their bodies from neck to feet. One had a shiny head covering. His companions had leather head coverings. The Sosabitom worked alongside Payomkawichum, many of whom were dressed in cloth of various colors. Noki wondered why they needed so much clothing.

"Some of them are from nearby tribes," Eti whispered.

"I think they are tribes from the coast," Noki said.

"What are they doing," Eti asked.

"Who? The Sosabitom?"

"Yes."

"Some are putting sticks in the ground," Noki said. "They are making lines in the dirt."

"Why do they wear so many layers of cloth?" Eti asked. "Do they get cold in the summer?"

"I don't know, Eti," Noki said, glancing at his father. Kwalah was watching the white men, his brows furrowed in thought. "Father, is our talking disturbing you?"

"No, you are asking the same questions I am thinking," Kwalah replied. "Perhaps it is customary among the Sosabitom to wear such things

An older white man walked with the aide of a long pole topped with something shiny. All of the other Sosabitom treated him with great deference. Noki assumed he was the chief among the white people. He and his followers wore their hair in a curious way, with no hair on top of their heads and a ring of hair all the way around. What amazed him the most was that each one of them had different color hair. Maybe Father knew why this was so.

"Maybe they come from different tribes," Kwalah suggested.

"But all of our people have the same color hair," Eti pointed out.

Kwalah shrugged. "Maybe the Sosabitom have more differences among their tribes than our people do."

"The red haired one seems to be an under chief," Eti observed.

The boys continued watching.

Noki watched them put up a house. It was bigger than the wamkish in his village. He had never seen a structure so large before. They were not here temporarily.

After a while the important ones stopped their work, and called the Payomkawichum to come to them. They knelt down and said prayers to their gods. The metal and leather-hatted ones took off their head coverings and Noki noticed the same variations in hair color. The Sosabitom were strange creatures, he thought.

"It's time to go," Kwalah whispered.

"Why do you think the s . . . strangers want to live here?" Eti asked.

"I don't know," Father replied thoughtfully as they continued back toward their camp.

Noki remembered something the shaman had told him and Koowut during the previous acorn-gathering season. "Kawawish said the Sosabitom make the people slaves, forcing them work until they die. Then they eat their flesh."

"D . . . do you think they do?" Eti's voice was touched with fear.

"I have heard they take slaves," Kwalah replied. "I don't know about the other."

"Most of the Payomkawichum had weapons," Noki pointed out.

"It would be stupid to give slaves bows and arrows," Eti said. "If I was a slave and I had a bow and arrow, I would k . . . kill my master and run away."

"I agree," Kwalah said.

The same thought occurred to Noki. Kawawish was the shaman and had terrible dealings with the Sosabitom, but perhaps the hearts of the white people had changed. The god, Ouiot had changed from good to evil. Was it conceivable these white men had changed from evil to good? Noki decided to leave the judgments to Captain Oomaqat, Kawawish and the elders of the tribe.

The trio hunted on the way back to camp. A half dozen small birds fell victim to their arrows.

"You are an excellent hunter!" Kwalah congratulated Eti.

"I can sneak up on anything," Eti boasted, holding up his three birds.

"Perhaps you can sneak up on the ancestors when they are doing the Dance of the Dead," Noki teased.

Eti grinned. "Someday, I will!"

After supper, Kwalah gave his report to the leaders of the tribe. A large fire accentuated the expressions of fear and awe on the faces of those who were listening. The boys sat beyond the fringes of the firelight and listened.

"The Sosabitom have come to stay this time," Oomaqat said. "To try to resist them would be like holding back the ocean with our hands."

"Their priest will poison the minds of our people. They will take our women and children and enslave them!" Kawawish exclaimed.

"I hear they feed the people during times of drought and famine," someone said after a short silence.

"You have to feed slaves in order for them to work!" Kawawish cried out. "Do you wish to become slaves because your bellies growl?"

"I hear they have marvelous animals that stand and wait for you to kill them," another person spoke.

"You are children!" Kawawish shouted. "They steal our gods!" There was muttering at the last statement. "They give you strange new gods."

"Will they come into the hills and canyons?" someone asked. Not even Kawawish answered.

Oomaqat spoke out, "No, they stay close to their ocean road."

"They can give sickness by looking at you," Kawawish added, his voice low, but distinct. There was another uneasy silence.

"Then we will stay away from them," Oomaqat declared.

"We must kill them before they kill us!" With that pronouncement, Kawawish stalked out of the meeting. Noki and Eti flattened against the rocks to avoid being trod upon. After the shaman had passed, Noki breathed a sigh of relief. Now would not have been a good time to attract the ire of the old man.

How could a person's gaze cause sickness, he wondered?

Eti put his mouth near Noki's ear. "The people by the river weren't sick."

Sometimes Noki thought it was uncanny how close their thoughts were. He motioned for his brother to follow him away from the group. They crept to their shelter, where Noki fell asleep dreaming of herds of deer that allowed him to walk right up to them and rabbits whose fur was black or red or brown or white.

Chapter 4

The next morning they began the last leg of the trip down the hills to the beach. They reached their destination by late morning. The women and children erected shelters while the men set about building reed boats. Noki and Eti walked north trying to find anything that could be added to the tribe's supplies for dinner.

"Over there, in the rocks, Eti," Noki cried, pointing toward a low, steep cliff. "We'll find plenty of nests there." Birds were flying about the rocks, darting toward the ocean and back, swooping like bats after insects.

"Let's see who can find the most eggs for Mother!" Eti challenged.

Stealth was not a prerequisite for this type of hunting. Noki's fingers and toes were sure and he soon found a feather-lined nest tucked in a crevice. Noki took one egg, leaving two to hatch, and placed it in a leather pouch slung over his shoulder. Both boys continued climbing, finding and collecting eggs as the angry birds swooped around their heads. Noki and Eti reached the top at the same time and flopped down on the thick grass, mindful of the eggs in their pouches.

"How many did you get, Noki?" Eti asked, panting.

"Four. How many did you get?"

"Five!"

"Good work...." Noki froze, hearing something unnatural. He looked across the meadow that stretched toward the eastern highlands. A group of Sosabitom and their Payomkawichum followers was coming their way. "Eti! Quick! Climb down." It was useless to hide; they had already been spotted, but at least Eti could get to safety.

"No, I will s . . . stay with y . . . y . . . you!" Eti declared.

Noki wasn't in the mood to argue. "Go on! Get out of here now!" he snapped. He was relieved to hear Eti moving back toward the cliff.

"Wait," one of the Payomkawichum called out. "We will not hurt you." His inflection indicated a distant tribe.

Noki stood, not wanting to meet these strangers groveling on the ground. He scrutinized them as they approached. The important one with the red hair was part of the group. With him were several of the people and a Sosabitom with a large leather hat.

"He is the priest here," one of the followers said, pointing to the important one, "Father Antonio wants to talk to you. I will translate his words."

Why is he called father? Noki studied the priest and was startled to see that his eyes were almost the color of the sky. The hair was strange and magical enough, but such eyes! Maybe this made him a very powerful priest. "What is it the priest wants?" he asked. It paid to be respectful to any priest.

"You came from the beach," the translator said. "Father Antonio wants to know if you saw eggs in the nests in the rocks."

Noki nodded.

"Good," the translator said. "He wanted to find some for his leader's breakfast."

"I have some," Eti said.

Noki frowned, irritated at his brother's recklessness. Eti pulled his pouch over his shoulder and handed it to the Sosabitom. The priest took the pouch and spoke to the boys.

"Father Antonio thanks you for your generosity. He says Father Presidente will be happy."

The priest pulled something from his own pouch and held it out to Eti. The boy took it, not touching the white man's fingers. He turned it around and around in his hands. "Wh . . . what is it?"

The Sosabitom must have guessed what Eti had said, because before the translator could say anything, he spoke again.

"A gift from Father Antonio," the translator said. "To help remember God and his Son."

Noki could see that Eti wanted to ask more questions, but he felt they had been there long enough. "We must go."

The priest moved his hands and Noki feared it might be a curse. He edged back toward the cliff, pulling Eti with him.

"Father Antonio leaves you a blessing. Something from the Holy God to bring good . . . fortune for you and your family," the translator explained. "He also says to come visit him in our new home." The Payomkawichum pointed toward the east.

A stranger was asking his god to bless his family? Noki mumbled a quick thank you as he began to climb down. If Sosabitom were so cruel, why was this one so friendly? The white priest had not tried to capture them. Indeed, he had given a gift. Noki shook his head, confused by what had happened. "I don't think we should say anything about this right now. And when we do, only to Mother and Father."

27

"Kawawish would not like it if he knew w . . . we had traded with a Sosab . . . bitom," Eti concurred.

"That's an understatement!"

"I gave away my p . . . pouch with the eggs," Eti added when they got to the bottom of the cliff.

Noki furrowed his brows in thought. That did complicate things a bit. "Just say you lost it," he finally said. That was at least partly true. He didn't know what the white priest would do with it. "I think we should throw this Sosabitom necklace into the surf."

"No!" Eti cried out. "The priest gave it to me for my eggs. It is my first trade."

Noki knew it was no use arguing. "I'll keep it in my pouch."

Eti felt the smooth wooden beads that hung around his neck as he took it off. He examined the small cross shape and exclaimed, "There is the shape of a man here!"

Noki leaned over him and studied the tiny figure.

"Is this the white man's god?" Eti asked softly.

"Since the priest left a blessing on us, I would guess so. I wonder why their god is like this? He doesn't look very powerful," Noki mused. Eti continued studying the figure. "It's getting late and we don't have much to show for our hunting. Let's see what we can find on the beach."

They were unable to catch any fish, but they harvested a fair number of clams. Noki made a seaweed basket for their catch and they headed back to the camp. By this time the sun was approaching the horizon, throwing bright light into their eyes.

Noki and Eti's birds and clams were happily accepted. The family ate on the beach. Noki and Eti lay on the still warm sand as the sky darkened. Seabirds flew overhead, swooping toward the waves for their last fish of the day.

The boys remained on the beach until the full darkness allowed them to watch the stars blanketing the sky. The Sky Path shone particularly bright.

"Eti," Tahmahwit called. Both boys stood and brushed the sand from their bodies.

"I'll beat you!" Eti sprinted toward the nearby campfires.

Tahmahwit didn't flinch as the boys stopped short in front of her, sliding in the sand. Atu suckled noisily at her breast, Father was smoking contentedly on his small soapstone pipe.

"You had fine hunting today," he said, taking a puff. "Despite the loss of the pouch."

"I am going to hunt for r . . . rabbits tomorrow to have skins to make a new p . . . pouch," Eti interjected.

"Good," Father said. The light-colored smoke from his pipe drifted lazily to the top of their lean-to like a soft and furry snake before it escaped into the darkness. When Father spoke again, his voice was barely audible. "What were the white men like?"

Noki looked at him in shock.

"Noki, you are an excellent weapon maker, but a bad storyteller," he said, serious, but not angry. "You should have found a safer place for your gift."

"We didn't want to have to answer Kawawish's questions," Noki replied in a low voice.

"Or feel his wrath." Kwalah took one more puff on his pipe and rose to his feet. "Let's take a walk on the beach."

When Eti started to follow, Father motioned him to stay in the camp. The younger boy didn't argue.

Waves lapped around their feet, the white foam glistening in the moonlight. The rhythmic, muted booming of the surf seemed to be echoing the beating of Noki's heart.

"You know Kawawish's reason for being afraid of these white men," Father began.

"Yes, but are all of the white men like those who killed his son? The white man today was very friendly."

Kwalah continued to walk on the beach, Noki following behind. "Walk beside me, my son. You are almost a man. You must walk a man's stride."

Noki complied, not saying anything.

"Kawawish also sees change."

"Change?" Noki asked.

"When we spied on the Sosabitom, you described how the Payomkawichum were wearing the clothes of the white men."

"Are they slaves?"

"I don't know, Noki," Kwalah said. "Tell me exactly what happened this afternoon."

Noki left nothing out. There was a long silence after his narrative.

"It's good Eti gave them the eggs," Kwalah finally said. "Since they are here to stay, it is good that whatever dealings we have with them are friendly." Father put his hand on Noki's shoulder. "You two did well. You have dealt fairly with them and there will be no claim against us or reason for them to come against us with weapons."

"If we all want friendship maybe the things that happened before will not happen to our people."

"Perhaps," Kwalah mused.

"Most of the time we get along with neighboring villages, Father. Why can't we get along with these Sosabitom?" Noki asked.

"We understand our neighbors and they us," Kwalah began. "They are like us. Their skin is the same, their eyes and hair are the same. We live much the same as they do. These newcomers are different. We do not know them nor they us. Already they set up their homes on other people's lands."

"So there is nothing we can do?"

"We live as Earth Mother and the gods would have us do. And hope."

There was nothing Noki could say, so he kept silent.

"Let's get back. We need to sleep. The hard work begins tomorrow."

In the days following, the problem of the white men was soon forgotten in the excitement of working with his father. Noki made and repaired spears and occasionally went out in the tule reed boats to try his skill with his weapons. After four days, seemingly endless racks of seal meat and fish stood drying in rows on the beach.

Near the middle of the fourth day, the skies became overcast and the men did not hunt. Only a few older boys, including Noki ventured out into the rough surf to fish. After he had fought the waves to the point of exhaustion, Noki rested on the sand.

"Noki, come with me," Eti whispered in his ear, interrupting Noki's dozing rest.

"What have you found now, Eti?" Noki mumbled without opening his eyes. "If it's a turtle, go play with it and let me rest."

"Not what, but who," Eti answered. Noki could hear smugness in his brother's voice.

Noki sat up, fully awake now. "Who?"

"Come on, or we won't b . . . be able to visit," Eti said, excited.

Noki could only guess that Eti had been visiting one of the nearby villages and had made a friend.

"Come on!" Eti said, pulling on Noki's arm.

"All right, I'm coming," he said with a laugh. He followed his brother along the shore to almost the same place they had climbed for eggs the first day. Eti went up a tiny winding footpath with the confidence of a deer; gathering eggs on his way. Soon they reached the top where Noki was surprised to see a young woman sitting on a rock, waiting for them. Or rather for Eti.

She studied Noki a moment before saying anything. "This is your brother, Eti?"

Noki was entranced. She was covered from the neck to below her knees in Sosabitom clothing. It did not resemble anything he had ever seen among his people. The clothing above her waist was white. The skirt was solid material, not apron-like like the skirts of the women in his village. It looked soft and he longed to touch it, but he didn't dare. It was a deep blue color like the sky in the late evening, but there were designs of red and white at the bottom.

It was obvious she was from the group with the Sosabitom priest, for no one else dressed like this. She laughed softly and he found it to be a musical sound. He didn't think she was any older than he was.

"I am Maria," she said in broken Payomkawichum language. "Named after the Holy Virgin Mother."

"Holy Virgin Mother?" Noki asked.

"That is the mother of Jesus," Eti interjected.

"Jesus?"

"The Son of God," Eti replied, showing the tiny figure on his beaded necklace.

Noki's eyes widened. "Chinigchinich had a son?" he asked.

Maria laughed again, but like before it wasn't derisive. "No, Noki, God the Father is not Chinigchinich. This is the one God. Jesus, the Son lived on Earth." She said something else that was mostly like a chant, but Noki couldn't understand what she was saying.

While he was interested in learning about her gods and how they were different from his gods, he was more interested in the white men and what their plans were. "You are with the white men by the river?"

"Yes."

"Maria and her mother come from the coast to the north," Eti said, not wanting to be left out.

"Yes, my mother and I came with some others from the Mission San Juan Capistrano a week ago," she explained, pointing in a direction that was almost directly up the coast. "My mother is good at cooking and sewing. I help her." Maria looked up at the sky. "I will have to go back soon. I am supposed to be gathering eggs and roots. Father Presidente likes eggs very much and Father Antonio has asked me to find any along the coast if I can. But it takes so long to walk here, I cannot stay."

"Mission. Is that what the Sosabitom home is called?" Noki asked, pointing in the direction of the new settlement.

"Yes," Maria replied. "It is the Mission San Luis Rey de Francia."

It seemed a very long name for something so small, but Noki said nothing. Eti reached into his pouch and pulled out the four eggs he had gathered, handing them to Maria.

She beamed. "Thank you, Eti."

Noki remembered a name she had said earlier. It was the same thing the red-haired priest had mentioned. "Father Presidente?"

"The white-haired bald one," Eti said, making motions of a fringe of hair around his head. "He is a priest, too."

So many priests, Noki thought. No wonder Kawawish had been unable to curse them. "They are erecting large houses," he said. "And staying," he added.

"Yes," she said. "And if you think these are big, you should see what has been built in San Juan Capistrano."

"Is the white man's tribe so large they need such monstrous places to live in?" Noki asked, augmenting with signs when Maria didn't understand.

She shook her head. "Some of the buildings are for praying to God in. The priests use them to teach us a better way to live," Maria explained.

"A better way to live?" Noki asked. "How can anything be better than the way we live now?"

"Oh, but there is, Noki. There are no disputes with our neighbors like before. There are no times of hunger. We are taught about the true God and how best to please Him."

Noki wondered if wearing the clothes was one of the ways the believers of this god pleased him. "What are these white priests like?" he asked. "Do they beat you?"

"Sometimes when someone has done a very bad thing, they will." She cocked her head to one side. "Don't your parents sometimes punish you for doing something wrong?"

"Yes, but Mother or Father have *never* beaten me," Noki declared.

"Some people do things that are very bad," she said. "But most of the priests I have met are kind. Father Antonio is very nice." She suddenly looked pensive. "I do not like the soldiers, though. Sometimes they look at me with eyes that are not kind. I stay away from them."

"The soldiers are the metal and leather-hat ones?"

"Yes," Maria said as she stood up. "I must go. I still need to find certain roots and don't want to walk in the dark."

Noki looked at the position of the sun, not realizing how long they had talked. "You will come back?"

"I don't know, but probably not. There is much to do at the new mission before we go home." Reaching out, Maria touched Noki on the hand. Her fingers were rough, but they felt pleasant. "Good-bye. May the Holy Mother watch over you both. Come visit the mission soon."

"Good-bye, Maria," Noki and Eti said together. When she left, Noki felt strange, as though he had lost something.

Chapter Five

Under the priests' directions, the valley sprouted buildings, large and small. "That will be a good place for the soldiers' barracks," the Father Presidente said, pointing to an area halfway between the site of the mission and the river.

Father de Lasuén was tireless. He worked alongside the others as they dug holes for posts, carried poles and tied mats on the roofs of the new buildings.

They walked to the spot he had indicated. "Twenty feet that way," Father de Lasuén said, pointing more to the south.

Antonio paced the distance and knelt down with another stake.

"There are still several hours of light," Father Presidente said. "If we work together we'll finish the enramada today. An enclosure open to the sky will be a suitable place for the Mass on the feast of St. Anthony of Padua."

Antonio eased himself from the ground. The muscles in his legs and back protested. "We'll begin right away, Father Presidente. Would you like to supervise from here?"

The Father Presidente snorted. "No. Antonio, I am not too old for this kind of work. When I can no longer work, it will be because I am dead," the older priest said. He grew more serious. "I feel the weight of my years. Soon that weight will take me beyond this mortal realm to dwell with the Blessed Mother of God and her Holy Son. Before you say anything, I am not being morbid, only pragmatic. God and the Savior have given me many wonderful years to serve them and our fellow men. There is much to rejoice over. I have seen the preaching take fire in this part of the world." An Indian brought each of them a cup of water. "I will rest for a short while. I want to talk to you about a few things."

Prior to their arrival, Father de Lasuén had talked of his vision for the new mission. In the past few days since their arrival there had been more discussions. Some had been around campfires late into the night when everyone else was asleep and others during meals or work. Topics had ranged from the making of adobe, bricks and tiles to various methods of teaching the Indians.

"I know you still have doubts as to your ability to head this mission."

Because of his vows of strict obedience, Antonio had never thought to question his calling, but he couldn't believe he had been chosen just because he worked hard and baptized many neophytes. "Yes, Father Presidente. I know there are others with much more experience."

"Yes, there are," Father de Lasuén said. "I considered all of them. However, I wanted more than an experienced missionary. I wanted someone dynamic, dedicated and energetic for this mission. Antonio, I want someone who can build lives. You have a God-given gift of drawing people to you. You have the dedication to bring souls into the Holy Mother Church and the heart to keep them here."

Antonio heard the Father Presidente's words, but had trouble assimilating them.

"If we don't get to work, we won't be able to dedicate this mission for you to use that gift."

Two days later Antonio took part in the High Mass of Saint Anthony of Padua, the ceremony that officially began the existence of the Mission San Luis Rey de Francia. With Father Juan Norberto, Antonio sang the holy chants that were part of the High Mass. Local Indians mingled with neophytes from the Mission San Juan Capistrano, sitting on the grass in the enramada. When the Te Deum Laudamus was sung to end the Mass, Antonio felt a deep gratitude that another stronghold of faith had been established. Later that afternoon he and the Father Presidente performed baptisms for more than fifty children. When he retired late that night, he was content.

As the days of hunting, gathering and trading on the beach progressed, Eti spent more and more time inland. He returned by suppertime, and had something to put into the dinner basket- a rabbit, bird, or squirrel, sometimes eggs or clams- but usually not enough to result from a full day's hunting. Eti said next to nothing about his whereabouts, behavior that caused Noki some concern. Up until now, Eti had confided all of his secrets to Noki.

When Captain Oomaqat announced they would be returning to their tribal lands in two days, Eti told Noki, "I have been visiting the village of the Sosabitom."

"What?" Noki cried. "Are you snake-bit or have you fallen head first from the cliffs?"

35

"Father Antonio is very n . . . nice and I was afraid to say anything because of K . . . K . . . Kawawish," Eti said in a rush. "So I went during the day when you were all working." There was a pause. "Mother knows."

"And she....?"

"She told me t . . . to be careful."

"When did you tell her?" Noki asked, suspecting it was not before he began his visits.

"I told her today." Eti refused to be cowed by Noki's disapproval. "I watched while they d . . . dedicated the land for their new village."

The word Eti used had a strange and foreign sound to it. "Dedicated? What is that?"

"A ceremony to make the l . . . land good for them."

"There is already a village nearby," Noki protested.

"This is d . . . different. This is a Mission." He said it like this mission was something special. "The old leader, Father de Lasuén, wore a fine white cape and said special words and burned special leaves that made white smoke. They sang wonderful songs. Later the old one put on his special cape again and said more special words and 'baptized' a group of Payomawichum. Some were younger than me."

"What is baptized?"

"Maria told me it was what someone did to belong to the white man's church to show you believe in their gods," Eti explained.

"You didn't do this, did you?" Noki said, looking over his shoulder to make sure no one was listening. "Let's go to the beach."

"No, of course I didn't!" His voice turned wistful. "But I would like to. Father Antonio and Father Juan tell wonderful stories about these gods. They are more powerful than Chinigchinich."

"No god is more powerful than Chinigchinich," Noki began, but then he stopped. Eti believed what he was telling him and Noki knew there was nothing he could say to the contrary. He tried a different track. "I am not going to say anything about this to anyone."

"Mother said she would go with me to the mission after we travel back to the hills."

While Noki agreed the Spanish priest seemed nice enough, he worried about becoming too close to these strangers. Kawawish might put a curse on their family if Eti joined this strange mission. They walked further along the beach and watched the foam encircle their ankles. The moonlight began to show through wispy clouds as they listened to the waves. A splashing in the

36

surf told Noki they weren't alone. He saw Koowut running toward them at his rumbling gait.

"Finally, I caught you two together," he said. "I was thinking you might be fighting with each other."

"I have been h . . . hunting each day," Eti said.

"Hunting?" Koowut teased. "You've brought back enough to feed your sister, if she wasn't still on your mother's milk." He laughed. "I know what you've been doing. You've been spying on the Sosabitom." He laughed, as though at a funny joke.

Eti's eyes widened in alarm. Noki signaled for him to calm down. "It would not surprise me if he was," Noki replied.

It was Koowut's turn to look surprised. "It's a long walk."

"Not so long for a runner," Noki replied. "You know how fast Eti is."

Koowut stopped laughing and asked. "Have you been spying on the white men?"

Eti took a breath and shook his head 'no.'

"I didn't think so. You're too little," Koowut told Eti.

Eti frowned, but another sign from Noki kept him quiet.

"Why don't we swim?" Koowut suggested. "We may not get another chance before we leave."

Eti brightened and soon the three boys were swimming in the waves.

When they were alone again, Eti nudged Noki. "You're smart."

"So are you."

The next day, when they were alone Eti told him what he had learned. It seemed a bit spotty and incomplete. Eti admitted he didn't understand everything the priests said. He spoke of the god named Jesus and the Holy Mother Mary.

Noki listened, but did not understand much of it. "Their god has the same name as the white priest?" he asked, incredulous. "That is like Kawawish having Chinigchinich's name."

"No . . . I mean their Father God is special. He does not need another name. The priests are teachers who have been chosen by their god to teach us."

"This Jesus, if he was so good, why would the people kill him," Noki asked.

Eti shook his head. "I wouldn't have, but I want you to go with me and Mother when I go next time."

Noki promised, if for no other reason than to make sure nothing happened to them in this mission village. Noki wished Tahmahwit had forbidden Eti to visit the Sosabitom, but he knew it would never happen. Mother had never been one to refuse Eti anything within reason. Noki knew she was curious, too. She had never seen white men and was impressed with Eti's stories of the Sosabitom and their new village.

Noki looked at it as knowing about one's enemy. At present, Father didn't know about the clandestine visits, and Noki wasn't going to tell him. As far as he was concerned, that was up to Eti or Mother.

The white priests were forgotten during the activity of rebuilding their village. According to custom, they did not go back to the place they had vacated, but went to a spot not too far from it. That allowed land where the old village lay to renew itself.

The women wove new mats for the dwellings and the men cut branches to form the frames of their new homes. The ground was scraped about six inches deep where the dwellings would be built. Kawawish supervised the construction of a new ceremonial house.

After several days of hard work, everything was finished. The baskets of dried fish and seal meat were stored away. The completion of the new sweathouse was celebrated by dancing and feasting that lasted late into the night. Noki spent time in the hills looking for more stones to make arrowheads and spear points.

One day Eti followed him out of the village. "Mother and I are going down to the mission tomorrow."

Noki had hoped Eti would forget such nonsense, but he should have known better. His brother, once having taken hold of an idea was like a badger with its prey. He could not be dissuaded.

Early the next morning, they set out, Eti, scampering ahead, his smooth wooden gift beads thumping against his chest. Mother had left Atu in the village with his aunt. Noki tried to walk with as much dignity as his father would. Mother walked beside him when the path was wide enough, her burden basket against her back, hanging by the rabbit fur strap that lay against her forehead. They were, as far as anyone in the village knew, going down the hill to gather reeds. Noki was not happy with this subterfuge, but his mother did not want the shaman to know where they were going, either.

"Mother, why are you letting Eti join this Sosabitom religion?"

Tahmahwit held her breath for a moment. "He believes the stories of the white priests and has accepted their gods. Eti says there are many things the same. Like the death of Ouiot."

"But, Mother, Ouiot was evil. This Jesus was supposed to be good."

"That is true, but their god gives laws, just as Chinigchinich has." Mother laid her hand on his shoulder. "I believe the Sosabitom may have changed since the days of our elder's youth. Eti talks constantly about how kind the blue-eyed priest is. I am going to see for myself and feel what is in my heart. I ask that you do the same."

"I am going to protect you and Eti."

It did not take them long to make the journey, and they soon found themselves standing beside the shallow river gazing at the women on their knees washing clothes. Noki half hoped that one of them would be Maria, but he was disappointed. One of the older women stood and walked across the river to greet them.

"Miiyuyam," the woman said, greeting them in their language, taking Tahmahwit's hands in hers.

"Thank you," Mother said, speaking for all of them. "We came to see the priest. I am Tahmahwit, these are my sons, Noki and Eti," she added.

"You are most welcome," the woman said, beckoning the trio to follow her. "The Fathers will be happy to see you." Curious children began to gather. Noki experienced a closed-in feeling he had never felt before.

All of the children, even the youngest, were clothed. The boys wore white cloth that covered their upper torsos and darker material that covered them from their waists to below their knees. They were barefoot and bareheaded. The little girls had on skirts and tops, much like what Maria had been wearing, but plainer. They were also barefoot. Noki stared for a moment, wondering how they could stand to wear so much clothing.

One of the children reached out and touched him on the upper leg. Noki jumped. They laughed and he felt his cheeks grow warm from embarrassment. He should be more brave, but all Noki wanted to do was run back into the hills. He wanted to be anywhere but among these people who were Payomkawichum, but weren't Payomkawichum.

The blue-eyed, red-haired priest came out of the largest building, and Noki stopped. Eti held up the beads and the priest greeted him in his own language. Noki didn't understand, but Eti did, because his younger brother quickly returned the greeting. He took Mother's hand and drew her over to the priest. Father Antonio. Noki remembered the name from their first meeting.

Mother pulled her cloak on. Noki hadn't noticed she had brought it. Eti must have told her of the white man's customs of dress.

When they walked into the largest building, Noki dashed over and peered in. He realized that while it was the size of a wamkish, this place was not open to the sky. Tahmahwit and Eti sat on the floor with a group of children, most about Eti's age, listening to the white priest tell stories. He used a great many gestures. Noki watched to make sure Eti and Mother were all right.

He now understood how the young eaglets felt when they were taken from the nests and caged for sacred ceremonies. It was not that these people threatened him in any way. They were all friendly, but they were so . . . different. The laughter of the children and the pleasant songs of this Father Antonio helped to ease his anxiety.

Eti jumped up from the group and ran to Noki. "Come Noki, I am b . . . being bap . . . tized. Me and Mother!" He was smiling from ear to ear. "You come and be baptized, too."

Noki shook his head. He did not believe in the Sosabitom gods and would not do anything to show loyalty to them. "This bap-tized; does it mean they make you stay?"

"No, Noki, it only m . . . means you b . . . believe in the great God, Jesus." He tugged on Noki's arm, his face shining in his excitement. "Mother is getting baptized, too," he repeated.

Eti was a child, he could be easily swayed, but Mother? Maybe she was doing it only because Eti was doing it. Noki shook his head.

"Come watch anyway," Eti coaxed. Noki followed his brother into the building. They walked to one side of the large room where Father Antonio stood with another priest. There was a large stone bowl on top of a stone in the shape of a tree trunk and Eti sat down before it at the blue-eyed priest's direction. The bowl was like the tamyush, the sacred stone bowl dug out of the ground only for special ceremonies. Noki gazed at the scene with rapt attention. There were several others sitting with Eti and Tahmahwit.

Father Antonio took a cloth from a young man standing next to him and put it over his head. It was a white cloth, decorated with bright yellow designs and it draped down around the priest's shoulders. He chanted words Noki couldn't understand, and beckoned one of the children to come closer to him. The child went to the priest, head bowed. The Sosabitom said some words and took a little of the water from the basin and sprinkled it over the boy's head. He did the same for each person sitting around the stone bowl, including Eti and his mother.

So this was baptism, Noki thought. When it was all over, Eti ran over to him. Noki studied his brother, but couldn't see anything different about him. "Are you all right?" Noki asked.

"Of course!" Eti said, with all the exuberance of a young boy who has tried something new and exciting.

Noki glanced over at his mother and saw the priest talking to her. Or rather signing to her. He wondered if the white man was trying to get her to stay. After a few more words and gestures, Father Antonio made the same blessing motion with his hands he had done for Noki and Eti when they met on the cliff.

Noki slipped out of the large room. Eti joined him. "I told you Father Antonio wouldn't do anything bad to us."

"Yes, you told me."

Someone handed Tahmahwit a leaf-wrapped packet.

"Did he try to make you stay, Mother?" Noki asked.

"Yes, but when I told him I must go, Father Antonio gave me a blessing.

As they walked toward home, Mother unwrapped the packet and sniffed the food inside. After tasting it, she handed each of the boys a piece. It was different, but not unpleasant.

Chapter Six

"He gave us a b . . . blessing from the Father God, Son God Jesus and the Holy Ghost," Eti said, excited.

"Holy Ghost?" Mother asked. "I didn't understand the talk about a ghost god."

Eti shook his head. "I do not understand all they said, but Father Antonio is nicer than Kawawish. I think his gods are, too."

"Then why do they make the people wear things that are not natural?" Noki asked.

"I don't know. I think the Sosabitom like clothes," Eti replied with a shrug of his shoulders.

Noki supposed if they wanted people living in their houses to wear more than was necessary, that was their business, but it still made little sense to him. Maybe these Spanish came from a place where it was cold all the time. Noki decided it was of no consequence. He had no intention of living among them.

When they were beyond sight of the Sosabitom mission Noki relaxed. He wondered at the strange power these newcomers held over the people. Could it be the power of their gods?

Mother stopped long enough to pull a smaller basket from the bundle on her back. Handing it to Eti, she instructed him to pick berries while she cut reeds. Noki pulled out his throwing stick and searched for prey. He was fortunate enough to kill a rabbit. It was not enough to show for a day of hunting, but they wouldn't be empty-handed when they returned to the village. It was almost sunset when they got back. Noki and Eti went to the stream to skin the rabbit. With speed developed from experience, Noki ran his knife at the places that would allow the easiest removal of an intact rabbit skin. After the cuts, he peeled the skin from the carcass, and handed the meat to Eti. Noki continued preparing the skin for tanning.

"You were down at the Sosabitom village, weren't you?" a harsh voice startled the boys. It was Kawawish. "You have been listening to the lies of the Spanish priests."

Noki stood up. In the deepening twilight, only the shaman's glittering eyes and gleaming teeth were distinct. What he dreaded had come to pass. Noki stood resolute. "We . . . we gathered."

"What—this?" the shaman asked, reaching around Noki and grabbing Eti's beads.

Eti was unprepared and stumbled forward. He grabbed the gift from Kawawish's grasp and pulled away from the old man.

"Take the meat to Mother, Eti," Noki commanded. When his brother had run out of sight, Noki turned back to Kawawish. He felt his tongue sticking to the roof of his mouth and his knees knocking together.

The shaman waved his feather-decorated eagle claw in Noki's face and the boy watched it in horrible fascination as it descended toward his chest. Kawawish's dark eyes bored into his and the boy felt himself giving way to fear. The eagle claws scraped his chest and it was the pain that brought him the strength to face the hard-eyed shaman.

"We went gathering," Noki managed to get out. His resolve ended up sounding weak and fearful.

Kawawish pounced on that weakness. "Your gathering was pitiful for three people who were gone all day."

Noki began to feel anger and he allowed it to overcome his fear. "Some days happen like that," Noki said, his voice more forceful. "We have enough for our dinner tonight."

"You would have more if you stayed away from the white men's settlement," the shaman growled.

The talons dug deeper into his chest but Noki refused to back away. He felt blood trickling down his chest. "The captain has not forbidden anyone to visit the Sosabitom."

Kawawish glared at him, his eyes cold. They were like pits, deep and dark. "No, but he refused to meet with them. And for good reason." He stuck his face almost into Noki's. "Do you not understand that the white men are death?" he asked, his voice almost a whisper. "Would you have them destroy us?" Kawawish paused. "There are the manhood ceremonies coming up. I would not be able to recommend a boy to manhood who disobeyed his elders. You are obstinate as your father was when he was a boy." Kawawish pulled the eagle foot away. Noki did not flinch and the shaman stalked away, muttering curses.

When Kawawish was gone, Noki closed his eyes. He let out a breath he didn't know he had been holding. When a hand rested on his shoulder,

Noki almost cried out. He jerked around and saw his father. Noki couldn't help himself, he threw his arms around Kwalah. He had defied the shaman.

"Come with me to the place of stone," Father said.

Noki looked at the bloody rabbit fur still clutched in his hand. He didn't remember holding it during the confrontation with the old man, but there it was, soft to the touch on one side, but still gory on the other. Noki wished for some of that softness in his life, but it seemed to be elusive.

Kwalah took the skin and studied it. "A fine job, son." He placed it in the stream, weighing it down with a large rock. "We'll get it on the way back."

They sat down on the rocky ledge outside of the cave where he had worked with his father before their trip to the ocean. Noki felt the warmth of the sun still in the stone.

"It is a dangerous thing to defy or anger the shaman, Noki," Father said as they watched the sky turn from dim twilight to star-sprinkled darkness. "But it wouldn't have mattered what you said to Kawawish, he would have still been angry."

"You know?"

"Yes, when Eti came back with the rabbit, crying about how Kawawish was going to kill you, your mother told me what you three had done," Kwalah said. "I thought Eti would not have had the initiative to do such a thing. I should have known better."

"I am sorry I didn't tell you sooner," Noki said in a soft voice.

"I wish you had," Father said, paused for a short while. "But if I had forbidden Eti to visit the white men, he would have gone anyway. You would have gone to protect him and things would be the same. You were very brave, Noki."

Noki could barely discern his father's profile in the darkness. The face was strong, but there was something in his father's voice that sounded unsure. "Could Kawawish keep me from the manhood ceremonies, Father?" Noki asked.

"He could try, but I don't think Oomaqat will change his mind. You have never been a trouble maker to anyone."

Noki breathed a sigh of relief.

"I think that is the least we need to worry about," Kwalah said.

"What do you mean, Father?"

"Only that so much is changing."

"You mean the Sosabitom?"

"Yes, and many other things with them." He didn't elaborate and they watched the stars glitter in the dark sky above them. Several coyotes howled in the distance. "We need to get back before your mother worries about us," Father said.

Noki thought it was too late for that, but he didn't say anything. He was grateful for the time alone with his father.

"Besides, I want some of that rabbit you killed," Father added.

They were soon inside their house, eating the roasted rabbit, fresh berries and porridge Mother had made from ground seeds. The trip to the white man's village was not discussed.

The following day, Noki tried to make arrow points, but he was unable to concentrate on the stones. Despite his father's reassurances, Noki worried about his future. Not being allowed to participate in the manhood rituals would be humiliating.

Several days later his father took him aside. "Noki, if Kawawish gives us too much trouble, we will go to the village of my brother's wife," he said. "They would welcome us."

Not long after that Eti demanded another trip to the mission. "No!" Noki retorted. "You have been bap-tized. That is enough to make all of the gods happy, ours and theirs."

"I want to learn more," Eti replied. "Besides, it has been a week and Father Antonio will be having the big Mass." His eyes showed his determination. "If you will not go with me, I will go alone."

"Kawawish is ready to put a curse on us as it is."

That took Eti back a moment. Kawawish ruled the tribe with fear. Noki pressed his advantage. "You would not want him to curse Mother or Father would you?"

"No." Eti's voice was sad. "But I made a promise to Father Antonio."

"What kind of promise?" Noki asked, suspicious.

"That I would come as often as I could so I could learn more about these new gods."

"Maybe when some time has gone by, Kawawish will forget and you can go," Noki suggested

Eti's shoulders sagged. "You're probably right," he said in a soft voice.

Eti did not go to the mission nor did he discuss it any more. Kawawish seemed assured that the white men were forgotten. All appeared to be back to normal.

Then early one morning, fourteen days after Eti's baptism, Noki saw his younger brother slip out of the village alone. He wouldn't have worried about it as Eti often went down to the stream to play, but the younger boy was acting different. He glanced over his shoulder every few paces, and finally cached his weapons under some rocks. *Perhaps Eti is only playing a game,* Noki thought. However, his brother continued on down the path they had taken to the mission. Muttering under his breath, Noki followed Eti.

As they neared the mission, he heard a strange noise. The noise repeated itself and seemed to be coming closer, but Noki still couldn't see what the creature was. Its call reverberated like the wolf's cry, but was less threatening, deeper and almost plaintive. In a strange way, it was like a deer.

Noki tried to catch a glimpse of Eti, while at the same time watching for the strange creature. Another low, mournful cry came from his left. A large horned beast pushed through the grass and cried out again. Noki stared slack-jawed at the animal for a few seconds before skittering back several paces. He tripped and fell back on his bottom. The huge black muzzle dripped saliva as it bent down to sniff him. Noki jerked back and the beast snorted and backed away as well.

Another of the beasts snorted behind him and Noki gathered himself to run. Then he heard laughter and saw a boy standing next to the large beast. He appeared to be about eight or nine summers old and wasn't the least bit afraid.

"You have nothing to be scared of. These are grass eaters and they have no young with them," the boy said to him.

"I know they are grass eaters," Noki retorted, embarrassed at being seen showing fear of tame creatures. "But even grass eaters have been known to trample a person when they are in a group."

"That is true," the boy answered. He was wearing clothes like everyone else in this place did.

Noki stood up and glanced toward the mission.

The boy noticed. "I was gathering the wandering ones before Mass started," he said. "Did you wish to attend?"

"No, but I will walk down part of the way."

"The younger one, he is your brother?"

"Yes," Noki said, keeping his eyes on the strange beasts. There were three of them and all were massive. The hair on their bodies was short, much like a deer's and their feet ended in cloven hooves. "What are these animals?"

"They are called cows."

Noki walked down the hill with the boy. The cows, walked ahead of them and when they hesitated, the boy prodded them with a stick or switched them on the backside. Their mammaries, unlike that of a deer's, hung low, swinging from side to side as they walked. It was no wonder these creatures needed the care of men.

"I'm Juanito," the boy said.

"I'm Noki. Do you live here?"

"Yes, with my mother and father. We came from San Juan Capistrano when the Father Presidente blessed this place.

Noki wondered if Juanito knew Maria. "You will stay here?" he asked.

"I think so," Juanito replied. "We like Father Antonio."

Suddenly a bell rang and Noki jumped. "What is that?"

Juanito laughed. "It's the mission bell. The priests use it to tell us when it's time to do different things."

"What is it telling you to do now?"

"It is time to go to Mass," Juan said with a laugh. "After a while, you get used to it, but I don't like doing things because a bell says to do it." He struck the closest cow with his switch and it lumbered to a slow trot. The other two cows increased their pace to match

The Sosabitom beasts did what they were told. It seemed the white men did, too.

They crossed the stream and climbed up the hill toward the mission. Noki stopped.

"I must go to Mass," Juanito said, his voice friendly. "Will you join me?"

"I will wait for my brother here," he replied.

Juanito shrugged his shoulders. "All right." Without another word, he turned toward the same large building where Eti had been baptized.

Noki sat under a tree, listening to the water, the songs of those inside the Spanish wamkish, and the chewing sounds of the cows. The music intrigued him. His people's songs were all one voice, matching if more than one person sang at the same time. No one sang anything different until the first song was over. Though it was different, it was soothing. Noki began to doze.

"You wouldn't be able to stalk a ground hog." Eti scolded him.

Noki's eyes jerked open and he saw Eti grinning down at him. He got up and brushed the leaves off his body, embarrassed by his lack of vigilance. "Are you saying you knew I was following?" he asked.

Eti scampered up the hill. "Of course I did. Now you can tell Father the Spanish priests will not kidnap me or make me a slave."

Noki snorted and dashed after Eti.

Eti slowed down and began laughing. Noki joined in. It didn't matter that Eti was likely to get into trouble for sneaking away from the village. He was safe, they were going home and the Sosabitom religion had not changed him.

Chapter Seven

They sat under a tree to catch their breath. "Was it worth going?" Noki asked. "Did you learn anything?"

"Their gods are very powerful, Noki."

"How?" Noki asked.

"They talked about the god, Jesus, changing water into a different kind of drink."

"Eti, you can put things in water to make it change."

"No, this was different. Father Antonio also told the story of Jesus' Father making lightning and thunder to frighten away the enemies of his people. I believe him. Their gods make me feel stronger than Chinigchinich ever did. It is said the Mother of Jesus can make those who have problems better, too," he said, his voice dropping to a whisper.

So, Noki thought, Eti was worried about the stuttering. What could he say? Father had once paid Kawawish the best parts of a deer to intercede with the gods for Eti. Not that Noki thought Eti was any less a person for his differences. Still, it bothered Eti. Noki wondered how the new gods could do something the old gods hadn't chosen to do?

They followed a track into a wooded canyon. Noki hoped they would be more successful this time. He didn't relish another confrontation with Kawawish.

They hunted throughout the remainder of the afternoon. There were deer in the area—but where? Some of the tracks were fresh, some hours old. Eti slipped to his side, signing excitedly and pointing to tracks on the trail ahead. A doe with a fawn and also a yearling. The doe was not for the taking, neither was the fawn, but a yearling would feed their family for many days.

After an hour of following the tracks, Eti signaled that the deer were in a thicket just ahead. Noki tested the breeze and moved to a point where he was downwind of the animals. He signaled Eti to move toward the thicket from the upwind side while he readied an arrow in his bow. He felt energy tighten his muscles and he willed himself to relax. There was slight noise and a young buck emerged, its eyes large and fearful, the nostrils flared. It sensed danger, wary of what was behind him. Noki could sense power in the creature.

Noki reminded himself of the need to focus. Never before had he shot a deer. He pulled back the bowstring, sighted and aimed. *Great One, let my arrow fly true, that our family may eat*, Noki thought. The young buck looked in his direction and Noki froze. New antlers knobbed the top of the animal's head and Noki could see the pulse of its heartbeat in its neck. As the buck turned, Noki released the arrow. Hearing the twang of the bowstring, the deer jerked its head around and began to spring away. In that split second the arrow reached its mark; a point behind the left shoulder. The buck gave one bound and collapsed to the ground.

The doe and her fawn leaped through the thicket and bounded up another trail. Eti burst through on their heels, saw the stricken deer and whooped with excitement and triumph. Noki stared in amazement for a few seconds before pulling out another arrow. It would not do to allow the animal that had sacrificed itself to suffer longer than needed.

The deer quivered and lay still. Noki was incredulous. He had actually killed a deer! Then he remembered what he should do. Noki knelt beside the deer and began to pray. "Chinigchinich, thank you for the gift of sookut, this deer, which has given itself for our needs." Noki pulled out his knife, and thanking the spirit of the deer for its sacrifice, bled it.

Noki considered the trip back to the village. He would have to construct something that would make it easier to drag the deer. As young as the buck was, it was much too large to carry on his shoulders. Noki selected two stout saplings and hacked them down with his knife. Eti twisted grasses into twine, which they used to tie the saplings together. They dragged the deer onto the makeshift travois.

"I have prepared the deer for the trip home, but we'll need help. Go and tell father what we have done. Don't say anything about the visit to the Sosabitom priests."

"Do you think I'm a babbling child?" Eti asked in disgust.

"No, of course not. Go get Father."

Twilight was settling when Noki heard Eti and Father's voices. Noki called out to them.

Soon his father was by his side, Chaht, his uncle, right behind him. In the waning light, Noki could see his father's eyes gleaming with pride.

"Eti told us you had a deer of such monstrous proportions that it would take six men to carry it," Chaht teased. "He said it was two men high and four long, its tracks sank deep into the earth from its weight and its dying cry shook all the leaves from the trees."

It was a good joke and Noki laughed with his uncle.

"It's a fine deer," Kwalah said. He clapped Noki on the shoulder. "You have done well. You've both done well. It is a gift from the gods that you made this kill after spending most of the day down with the Sosabitom."

Noki was beginning to think he couldn't keep any secrets from his father.

"Your mother told me when I couldn't find you at the quarry," Kwalah explained.

"Jesus and the Holy Virgin are watching out for us," Eti added.

Father frowned. "We will not talk of that now."

Eti wisely obeyed.

As they followed Chaht, Noki began wondering. If he was sure they were helped to find the deer by the ancient gods of the people and Eti was sure his gods were responsible for this, who was right? *Whose gods were real? Which ones were the more powerful ones? Could all the gods be living together in the skies? No, Eti said the priests told him the old gods were false. Chinigchinich false? Never!* With that thought, Noki put the argument out of his mind and concentrated on walking the dark trail toward the village behind the buck deer he and Eti had ambushed. With little effort, Chaht pulled the deer to within a short distance of the village.

"My son, can you pull it the rest of the way?" Father asked.

"Yes."

"Good. Take your kill into the village as befits a successful hunter," he said.

Noki did as Kwalah suggested, grateful for the honor his father was giving him. With Kwalah walking on one side and his uncle on the other and Eti strutting behind, he pulled the deer through the village. People left their homes and cook fires to see what they brought.

"My son Noki, killed this fine buck with one shot," Kwalah announced publicly, his voice loud enough to echo through the village.

"Eti helped me ambush it," Noki added.

Mother clapped her hands in celebration before she pulled out her knife and cut off a back haunch. "Take this to the widow Mahkah," she told Noki.

Noki did not doubt that the other haunch would go to Kawawish. He, as the village's spiritual leader, usually received gifts of food. Noki was glad he had not been asked to deliver that gift.

Despite the fact Father had talked a great deal to Eti about going off alone to the white man's village, the young boy was determined to visit the blue-eyed priest and hear the stories of the white man's gods. Eti snuck away and again Noki accompanied him. On the return trip, they did not find any game other than two rabbits. Noki took the rabbits to the stream to dress them.

"Noki." It was Koowut.

"Koowut, I have not seen you for a long while."

"No wonder. Sneaking off down the hill after your brother."

Noki looked around for any eavesdroppers.

"I made sure no one else was around," Koowut assured him.

"Thank you," Noki replied. "I am worried about Eti and Mother."

"I thought maybe your mother might have done the white man joining ceremony, too."

"Yes, but at least Mother hasn't wanted to go back," Noki confided.

Koowut lowered his voice. "I have heard Kawawish is going to curse your family."

"But why?"

"He's afraid if others hear of your friendliness with the white men, they will want to be friends with them, too. Already there is talk of trading with the Sosabitom to get their knives and cooking pots."

"But Eti is just a boy!"

"I know that, but you know how Kawawish hates the white men. "Some whisper he's already laid a curse on your family."

"No!" Despite Kawawish's ineffectiveness at cursing the white men, the boy knew the shaman still had power. Last year a man in another village cheated Oomaqat in trade and Kawawish laid a curse on him. Noki heard the man had died.

One of the rabbits lay limp in his hands. "Father and I have not been baptized."

"It does not matter. The people will see that Kawawish is still powerful if one of your family gets sick," Koowut pointed out.

Noki felt a surge of anger. "If anyone dies because of Kawawish's cursing...."

"What?" Koowut interrupted. "What can a boy do against someone like a shaman?"

Noki's looked down at the ground. "I don't know," he said in a low voice.

"Pray to the gods and ask for their forgiveness," Koowut suggested. "Hope Kawawish is unsuccessful. I will do the same."

"Thank you, Koowut."

The next several days, Noki watched everyone, checking for signs of a successful curse. Noki went into the hills to pray. He did all the things that might please the gods.

For almost a week, nothing happened, and then one morning, Eti complained of being tired. He became feverish and could not stand to be in the sun. Mother prepared all of the remedies she could think of, but still Eti worsened. Spots appeared all over his body. The older women lamented about the spotted sickness that had killed many people years before. Father decided to ask Kawawish to help fight the sickness.

"Father," Noki said, deciding Kwalah needed to know what Koowut had told him.

"Not now, my son," Kwalah said, his voice tight with worry.

"Father, Kawawish put a curse on our family," Noki blurted out.

His brow furrowed in thought. "I heard the rumor, but there is nothing to be done but to ask Kawawish to attend Eti. Perhaps what we heard was wrong. We will take some meat as a gift."

Noki wasn't sure about anything right now. He helped his father gather baskets of dried meat, seeds and roots. They carried them to the shaman's house.

When they got there, he heard chanting from inside. Kwalah scratched on the deer hide cover. They stood quietly while the chanting continued. After what seemed an eternity, Kawawish's wife poked her head though the doorway. Father handed her the baskets and waited while she examined their offering. Finally, she pointed inside. Noki and Kwalah went into the dim, smoke-filled home.

Kawawish had on his feathered headdress, his ceremonial skirt woven with rabbit fur, feathers and pounded, dyed reeds. Around his neck were several necklaces, one strung with bear and puma claws, one with eagle feet and another with a variety of shells. The red-gold glow of the fire made him appear like an animal ready to leap on them with claws and fangs.

"We have brought gifts, great shaman of Chinigchinich," Father said, his voice deferential. He knelt down before the shaman and Noki followed suit.

Kawawish scowled at them. "You have offended Chinigchinich by joining with the Sosabitom gods," Kawawish growled.

"My youngest son is sick with a spotted fever. Nothing we can do is helping him."

"Of course not," Kawawish snarled. "It's the curse of the white man."

"You are more powerful than the white men, Kawawish. Take the curse from him," Kwalah pleaded.

Kawawish pointed a gnarled finger at them. "You have angered the gods. Your family has joined with the Sosabitom. I warned you these white men are death and you have disregarded that warning. Now you wish me to take this curse away?"

"Eti joined them because he liked the stories. He was taken with the white man's gifts."

"Is he not your son? Can you not control your own children and women?"

"Show the gods of the Sosabitom that you are more powerful," Kwalah persisted.

Noki could hear the desperation in his father's voice. His heart was squeezed with fear at the thought his little brother might die.

"Chinigchinich told me not to touch those who have joined the white men. He told me he will punish you!"

After the space of several heartbeats, Kwalah implored the shaman one last time. "You will not help one of the people? You will not help a child?"

"I will not touch one who has taken the white men's gods into his heart."

"Come, Noki," Kwalah said in a shaky voice. They went back to their own house. Those not out gathering or hunting moved out of their way. After all, Noki thought bitterly, who would want to incur the wrath of the shaman or the gods? Kwalah ducked through the opening of their house and Noki followed right behind. Mother's eyes looked hopeful until she saw her husband's face. She began to moan and cry, holding Eti to her chest and rocking as she cried. He was limp, the soft rattling of his breathing telling them the boy was still alive.

Noki knelt beside his mother and reached out to touch Eti. There was still life, but Noki knew in his heart it would soon be gone. Atu sat in the corner, sucking on one fist and then on the other, her eyes wide and fearful. Anger filled his heart. Some of it was directed to the white men, but most at Kawawish. "He has no power," he declared.

"What?" his father asked, kneeling down beside him. His fingers traced the line of his youngest son's jaw.

"Kawawish," Noki said. "He is afraid."

"Do not say such things," Mother admonished.

"Mother, Eti told me that to be baptized was the same as serving the white men's gods"

"I did it to please Eti," Mother cried. "And to make sure the baptizing would not hurt him. I still worship the gods of our people." She rocked back and forth.

"Kawawish put a curse on us," Father murmured.

Eti moaned. "Father Antonio...."

Tahmahwit put a little clay container to Eti's lips and the boy drank a swallow or two of water before sinking back into deeper sleep.

"He keeps calling for the white priest," Mother said. "And for the white men's gods."

Is the Spanish priest powerful enough to take the sickness away? "I will go and get Father Antonio," Noki declared. "He will come and take the sickness away."

"He will never come," Father replied in a wooden voice. "The white men stay in their own villages."

"I must try, Father. Eti will die without help. Maybe the white priest's power is enough to take the sickness away without leaving his own village."

Mother looked hopeful. "Go and ask, my son. Go quickly."

Kwalah said, "Be careful, Noki."

Noki pulled down a woven loincloth. He didn't want to do anything to offend the white priest. "When Eti awakens, tell him where I have gone," he said.

"Yes. Please hurry," Mother whispered.

"I will." Noki began his journey to the mission. As he ran down the path, he let hope fill some of the places where anger and despair were dwelling.

Chapter Eight

Antonio knelt in front of the simple wooden cross hanging on the adobe wall above his bed. A single candle, slightly crooked in a cracked pottery dish illuminated a tiny corner of the room. He didn't need illumination; at least not that kind of illumination. He needed guidance. Antonio needed to know how to reach the Indians living up in the hills. Some had come to the mission out of curiosity, but most stayed away. They were out of sight and out of reach. He had been fortunate the villagers close to the mission accepted the teachings. The chiefs were willing listeners and most had already been baptized. The members of their villages had followed suit.

"Most Holy Virgin, intercede, please, so I may reach these souls that are so precious to thy Blessed Son, and to me," he prayed fervently as the candle flickered and caused shadows to dance on the newly built adobe walls.

He heard a soft sighing that had nothing to do with the breeze blowing in from the ocean. It was like the passage of a wraith, but Antonio felt this was something alive, not dead. He continued to pray, but mostly he listened. A soft footfall. Another one and the faint whispering of breath.

He had a visitor. Antonio wondered if it was one of his neophytes coming to ask for a blessing or for help with a problem. No, if it had been a baptized Indian, he would have come openly, announcing himself, if by no other way than by scratching on the outside of his mat covered doorframe. This was someone who had not been here before.

He heard the sound of a stone knife being slid out of its sheath. Someone was here to kill him! He could not allow that! He had been sent here for a purpose. Antonio made no betraying move, continuing in his prayers on the hard-packed dirt floor next to his small cot.

The intruder came closer; Antonio judged him to be a few feet behind him. The priest jumped up, ready to fight for his life. In front of him stood a young Indian man, barely out of childhood, crouched with a knife in his hand. He was not one of the neophytes of the mission.

The boy-man jumped back, his eyes wide with fright. He looked like a wild deer, ready to run. Antonio felt there was something important about this boy. He could not let him leave without talking to him.

"Stop!" he called out in his language and then in the young man's. The boy started in surprise, still ready to run. "Do you understand me?" Antonio asked.

"A little," the Indian said, making a motion with his fingers.

"I will not hurt you," Antonio told the boy; also signing a greeting of good will.

The Indian studied him.

"Do you understand what I said? You can put your knife away," Antonio assured him.

The boy looked down at his hands, almost in surprise, and put the knife away. "You are Holy Father." It was a statement, not a question. He peered closely at the priest in the dim light as though picking out discerning features. "Father Antonio?" he asked. His eyes flicked around the room as though it might close in and swallow him.

The boy knew him? He seemed familiar, but Antonio couldn't place him. The priest watched the shadows dance across the Indian's almost naked body. The boy was lean and lithe in appearance. A light sheen of sweat told Antonio he had run all the way to the mission from his village. His shoulder length hair was tied back with a leather thong. An animal skin belt covered his loins and a dark stone hung on a leather thong around his neck.

"I am not the Holy Father," Antonio said. "The Pope lives a far distance away." He saw the look of incomprehension on the boy's face and berated himself. This boy didn't know a thing about the Pope or Rome. He tried again. "I am the Holy Father's helper. I am Father Antonio."

The boy said nothing for a moment. His eyes, in the dim light of the sputtering candle showed him to be thinking furiously. "You, Father Antonio. Brother's teacher." The words were a mixture of barely learned Spanish and the local Indian language.

"Yes, I am." He motioned for the boy to sit down, but the Indian remained standing.

"Eti wants you. I, Noki."

"Welcome, Noki." Antonio wondered for a moment if the boy had come to be baptized, but realized from the serious expression there was another reason for Noki's presence.

The boy shook his head. "You come see Eti."

"Eti?"

"My brother. He come here. Baptized," Noki made the motions of water being sprinkled on his head. "By you."

"Oh, you want to see him," Antonio said, thinking this Eti was one of the Indians living on the mission grounds.

The boy was exasperated. "No, Eti in village. Sick. Asked for Father Antonio. You."

Antonio didn't remember an Eti, but most neophytes received new names when they were baptized, unless they were old enough to say otherwise, or their parents made special requests. "Did your brother tell you his new name? His baptized name?"

"He say you call him 'Ho-sef'," Noki replied.

Antonio knew who Noki's brother was. Eti had come with his mother to be baptized. Noki had been there, skulking in the corners. "Eti is sick?"

"Yes. Hot—coughing, red. He wants *you*."

There was the possibility this was a clever plan of a group of Indians to kill him and destroy the mission, but in that instant Antonio knew this was no trick. Noki was here because he was desperate. Because it was not a trick, he would do what he had been called to do—serve. "Noki, it is almost dark, but if you will lead me, I will come to see your brother," Antonio said.

"I take you."

Antonio breathed a quick prayer and gathered his accoutrements for last rites, in case, God forbid, the boy was too far-gone. Pulling his cincture a bit tighter around his waist, Antonio picked up his staff and broad brimmed hat. He stepped out of his corner room and into the soft twilight of the late evening.

"Come," Noki urged, his voice anxious.

Travel usually took place during the daylight hours, because unknown paths held dangers. Even the neophytes who had lived their lives in this territory and knew the land intimately, did not often go far from their villages at night. The old cougar seeking an easy meal, the unseen snake that might be trod upon in the dark, and the loose stones easily slipped on, all were dangers to eyes that could not see as well at night. The moon would soon be rising and Antonio knew it was almost full. That would help them.

"Father Antonio!" Father José Faura, the padre assigned to help build the mission, called out to him.

"Yes, Father José," Antonio turned as the priest rushed out of the doorway. The younger man glanced nervously at the almost naked Indian.

"Father, it is late."

"Yes, I know," Antonio replied to the obvious.

"Are you going far?"

"I am going with this boy to his village," Antonio answered in a calm voice. "I don't know how far it will be. Probably not more than a league. The boy's brother, one of our newly baptized neophytes, is ill." Antonio felt a great affinity for this earnest follower of God, but the young priest was having a hard time acclimatizing to this remote post. "Don't worry. I will be safe. If I am not back in time, you can say the Mass tomorrow morning."

"Are you sure?" Father José asked, his rosary beads clicking in nervous fingers.

"Yes, I feel safe with our brother here." Behind him, he heard Noki shuffling from one foot to the other and knew the young man wished to be away. "You can help by lighting a candle for our young neophyte, Josef," he added.

"I will be sure to do that, Father Antonio. Vaya con Dios."

"Thank you, brother. Thank you," Antonio said. He turned and motioned for Noki to lead the way.

They crossed the boisterous little river, smaller in this dry season, stepping on well-placed stones. Antonio shivered as water splashed over his toes. It was the middle of August, but the water was chilly.

As they traveled farther from the mission, Antonio studied the dark path at his feet, looking up often to watch the back of the young man leading him away from the safe sanctuary of his new home.

They continued up a path and into the hills. The young man's steps were sure and swift and the priest tried to emulate their placement. Even so, early in their journey Antonio stumbled on a loose rock, losing his staff. He fell to one knee as he clutched at the small pouch holding a vial of holy oil. Noki stopped, but did not offer to help. He seemed to regard Antonio with pity. "I am all right," Antonio said, rubbing his knee as he got to his feet. "Continue."

The way became steeper and Antonio had to grasp the bottom of his habit in one hand to keep from tripping. At a difficult place, where the priest had to practically climb up the side of the incline, Noki stopped. After a moment's hesitation, the Indian reached out and offered his hand. Antonio gratefully accepted the help and realized Noki had strength belying his size and age.

He also realized this boy, who had spent most of his time at the mission standing in dark corners, had quickly picked up the Spanish language. "Thank you, Noki," he panted.

The boy touched the gray woolen material. "Clothes bad. Hard to walk," was all Noki said. He pointed to his own almost naked body. "Walk easy."

Antonio thought a minute as he caught his breath. How did he explain his clothing to someone used to wearing almost nothing? "These clothes are good . . . for God."

"God make you wear?" Noki asked, slowing a little. He must have realized the priest would not make it to his village if he continued at such a furious pace.

"Yes," Antonio said.

Noki frowned. "God makes Father Antonio wear bad clothes. God not like priests?"

"I wear these," he began, pointing to his habit. "Everyone knows I help God."

Noki looked at the moon and back at Antonio, nodding. "You Father. You wear...." He touched Antonio's habit. "I not Father. I wear...." And he pointed to the deerskin loincloth.

"Yes, Noki," Antonio replied.

The path went through a small aroyo, one shadowed from the light of the moon, but Noki led the way with the assurance of one who knew these paths well, and Antonio trusted him. They came to a flat area filled with grass. The moon showed a small herd of deer grazing in the distance. In unison, all of the creatures lifted their heads and bounded away.

The moon illuminated his way clearly here and Antonio noted the trodden grass through the middle of the meadow. He hoped it meant they were approaching Noki's village.

Noki picked up the speed again as they walked through the meadow.

Antonio thought of Noki's sick brother. The Indian said he was hot and having problems breathing. *Measles?* Hopefully, the boy was strong enough to withstand it and would only need rest and medicine to recover. The coughing worried him. Was Eti at the beginning of the illness or at the end? If at the end, the coughing was not a good sign. Antonio fingered the rosary and prayed they would find Eti alive and able to recover.

The pair heard sounds of the village well before they arrived. The first thing that came to Antonio's ears was a faint wailing, the sound of several women's voices. The priest's heart sank, having heard Indian women crying out their grief at the death of a loved one before. Ahead of him, Noki stopped so abruptly that Antonio almost ran into him. Laying his hand on Noki's shoulder, he asked, "What is it, my son?" The priest hoped there was another reason for the sound.

"Death," Noki replied in his own language as he broke into a run, leaving Antonio alone in the darkness.

Chapter Nine

Antonio continued on, using the sound of the women's voices as his guide. The glow of several campfires revealed figures moving about, their shadowy forms stark and nebulous at the same time. He tried to figure out where Noki had gone. An older woman gawked at him, her eyes made larger than normal by the reflection of the flames. She said something he couldn't understand.

Men came out of the nearest homes and stood shoulder to shoulder as though forming a wall. They were naked, their muscles sinewy and strong. In each man's hands were different kinds of weapons. Their faces were unfriendly. Antonio felt anxiety rising and his fingers touched the knotted rope cincture. He followed its length to the rosary hanging at the end. The smooth wooden beads had a calming effect as he rubbed them.

"Miiyuyam," he greeted the assembled group. "I am here with Noki. To see Jo . . . Eti."

None of the men said anything. Antonio stepped forward a pace, but the men did not move. "Noki," he repeated. "Eti." None of the men moved. "In the name of God and the Holy Virgin, let me pass."

Another Indian pushed through the group of men and stopped several feet in front of Antonio. He was older and wore a short cloak made of feathers and fur. Animal claw necklaces hung around his neck and low on his chest. He snarled something Antonio could not understand, but his anger was clear.

The light of a campfire gave the Indian's features a ghastly appearance. The eyes were dark pits, a feathered headdress swept up on either side of his head like horns and his thin arms had a skeletal appearance. This had to be the village shaman.

Antonio grasped the cross at the end of his rosary, holding it up in front of his chest. He would not cower before this man. The feel of the silver and wood crucifix was warm, dispelling the cold evil he felt from the shaman.

Antonio intoned a prayer of protection, asking the Virgin to intercede in his behalf. A fire crackled behind him; another fire flickered behind the wall of men, making weird shadows dance against a house within its light. Antonio ignored these distractions. He gazed into the Indian's eyes. His hands moved from the cross to the rosary beads. They clicked together as he

62

mentally recited several Hail Mary's. The Indian dropped his gaze to Antonio's hands.

All of the Indians stared at the crucifix that caught the red glow of the fire. The metal reflected a distorted image of the shaman. Realizing what it was that had caught and held the gaze of the men, Antonio raised the cross, making sure it continued to reflect the flames. The shaman backed up, almost bumping into the man behind him and Antonio stepped forward.

The old man cursed and spat on the ground at Antonio's feet. He shook what appeared to be a feather-decorated club in his face, pushed past the priest, and disappeared into the darkness.

The loud cries of sorrow increased in volume. "Eti?" Antonio asked one of the men. The Indian beckoned him to follow. He motioned for the others to step aside and ducked through a mat-covered doorway.

Antonio followed him. He felt stifling heat enveloping him like a heavy blanket. A large basket hung from the center poles over the fire. In it, water bubbled, steam billowing from its depths. Antonio saw Noki and several others bending over a still form lying on the ground.

"Father Antonio!" Eti's mother cried. She said something he didn't understand, but she made room for him, moving near a man whom he assumed was Eti's father.

Antonio knelt beside the still form. His hand hovered over Eti's mouth and nose. There was no breath. Gently, Antonio touched the boy's cheek. It was the measles, as he had feared. "I am so sorry," he told the parents.

Antonio remembered Eti as the fearless, inquisitive child who peered at the statues of ivory and painted wood, stared at his alb and amice, the gown and head cloth used for special mass. Eti had fingered the cincture around Antonio's waist and held the rosary, gently rubbing each of the polished beads. Antonio remembered when this outlying pair joined the Holy Church. He blinked the sting of tears away.

With a delicate touch, Antonio brushed a strand of hair away from the boy's face. He would ensure Eti's last rites. Though dead, unable to give confession or take the sacrament for the last time, death had been such a short time ago, the spirit of this boy would be lingering. He turned to the parents. "May I...." Antonio pantomimed what he intended to do.

"Eti good," she said, tears streaming down her face. "Send...." She motioned toward the sky.

"Yes." Taking off his hat and opening up his pouch, Antonio pulled out the *estola*, the ceremonial cloth. He kissed it and placed it around his neck. Whispering a prayer, he pulled out and opened the small bottle and touched the index finger of his right hand to the holy oil it contained. He dabbed the oil on the boy's eyelids, his ears, nose, mouth, hands and feet. "May this anointing take away any sins committed; those things which the eyes should not have seen, which the ears should not have heard, things that should not have been said, things better left untouched and unvisited. May our Lord Jesus make you his," he said in Latin, ending with the sign of the cross. When he looked up, he saw that the grieving father had been watching intently. "I am sorry I did not get here sooner," he said. "I have done what I could to help him leave this life in peace," he added, using hand signs to convey his words.

The woman's cheeks glistened with fresh tears. She bowed her head, lightly touched the hem of his habit. "Graciás."

"I will say a mass for him and for the rest of you," Antonio told her, lightly touching her on the shoulder.

The woman began signing to Antonio while she spoke. "Husband thanks you. Eti wanted you to come. Pray to Jesus for him. Eti with Jesus now?"

"Yes, my child," Antonio reassured her as best he could. Tears ran down the woman cheeks, but the husband's features were stolid. He said something else in his language.

"Kwalah glad you came to Eti. He thinks better you should leave now. We prepare Eti to go to the Starry Path," she said.

"I can bury Eti in the mission cemetery," Antonio offered. For a moment nobody said anything.

She shook her head. "We take care of Eti, Padre. Thank you."

"It is all right, my child. You bury him here and I will pray for his soul," Antonio told her.

"Sorry not giving you . . . bed, food."

"That is all right," Antonio assured her. He put his things away. "God bless you," he said and left. Most of the tribe was standing nearby. He blessed them and strode out of the village. No one bothered him.

When he was away from the village, Antonio stopped to get his bearings. He knew he couldn't make it all the way to the mission tonight. If he could find a tree he could climb, that would be safe enough until morning.

In the moonlight, the path was fairly easy to follow. He soon found the rocky slope. Feeling with his feet, and groping for handholds among the rocks, Antonio made his way down. A rustling at the bottom of the arroyo startled him and he slipped on a loose stone. He fell a few feet before catching himself. His knee began throbbing again.

The rustling took the shape of a wary skunk and Antonio remained stock-still. It dug under rocks for what seemed an interminable time, looking for something to eat. Finally, it meandered away.

Antonio was more careful now and it took him much longer to get down the path. When he came to a meadow, he saw, not more than twenty feet away, a large oak tree. Its branches spread perpendicular from the trunk. Howling that sounded too close for comfort sent the priest scurrying up the tree. While St. Francis was the patron saint of animals and he *was* a Franciscan, Antonio didn't think any hungry beasts out here would worry about that. A Franciscan would taste as good to a wolf as a Jesuit.

The trunk was huge and gnarled, much larger around than his outstretched arms could measure. After some effort, Antonio found himself sitting on a wide limb, his back against the trunk. When the sun rose in the morning, he was sure he could make his way back to the mission.

While sitting on his rough bark 'chair', Antonio thought of his visit to the village. In Mexico City, he had been told the Indians were lazy and the only way to make them *gente de razón* or 'people of reason' was to force them to live at the missions where they would be under the influence of the priests twenty-four hours a day. That appalled him. Still the problem remained. If they weren't willing to come to him, what could he do to give them salvation?

Tonight, he had gone to an outlying village, trusting to God it was the right thing. Then it dawned on him. Missionaries had come here all the way from Spain. What were a few more leagues to bring the saving ordinances to the villages of these Indians? Now he knew what God wanted him to do! He would take the gospel to the Indians wherever they were, even the remote villages.

Satisfied, Antonio rubbed his sore knee and settled into the fork of the tree to go to sleep. He shivered in the chill air, but was so tired he couldn't stay awake.

When he woke up, Antonio yawned and stretched. The sun was shining in his face and he realized he had slept later than normal. A slight rustling below caused him to look down. Noki was sitting at the base of the tree; a tiny fire smoldering at his feet.

Chapter Ten

"Why did you follow me?" Antonio asked, climbing out of the tree. He brushed himself off.

"Tahmahwit say watch. Make sure you find path to mission or Jesus God be angry," Noki replied. "I left you in village. That was bad." Intricate signs accompanied the word, but Antonio was able to understand.

"Tahmahwit. Is that your mother's name?"

"Yes," Noki told the priest.

"Noki, I understand why you left me in the village," Antonio reassured the boy. "Nothing bad happened to me."

"Mother say you came. Kawawish say you not come."

Antonio assumed Kawawish was the Indian priest. The shaman's belief he wouldn't come was justified. There was no precedent for any priest making a visit to an outlaying village in the middle of the night. So many things could have happened, Antonio realized now, but he had been protected. He had learned a way to teach the people here. "He was wrong, I did come," Antonio said. In the silence that followed his statement, he looked around the meadow. "Is there a stream nearby?"

"I show you," Noki said.

"Graciás, Noki." They walked a few moments in silence. "I'm sorry about Eti. I wish I could have helped him."

"Mother say you call Jesus God. Make Eti well, but it was not . . . to be. He died." Noki hung his head. "Run, not fast enough."

Pity welled up in Antonio's heart. "Noki, do not blame yourself. If I had gotten to him earlier, he may still have died."

"Jesus God and Father God not heal Eti? Eti not good enough?"

"Eti was a good boy. He did what God wanted him to do, but if he had finished his time here on Earth...."

"What you mean—finish his time?" Noki asked, his brow furrowed in thought.

Antonio thought this was getting deeper than he could properly explain to this unhappy young man. He tried to find the right signs to go with the words. "It means if you have done everything in life...." he explained.

"You priest of Jesus God. You heal followers of Jesus." Noki sat down on the bank, waiting for the priest to say something.

Antonio sat down beside him, letting the cold water splash over his feet. "Kawawish is your people's priest?"

"Yes, shaman hears Mother Earth, Chinigchinich and other gods. He speaks to them. He tells us what gods say."

"Did he try to save Eti?"

"No, Eti bap-tized."

Antonio was disgusted with the shaman's neglect of the sick child. "Does he try to save other people in your rancheria who are sick?"

"Yes."

"Do all the sick live?"

Noki thought for a moment. "No, sometimes sick person dies."

"Why?"

"Someone wants them…." Noki motioned to the sky above him.

Antonio figured that Noki was referring to the Indian notion of heaven. "Yes, Noki. It is the same for me. I cannot save everyone because God may want him in Heaven."

"So Father God and Jesus in Heaven are like Earth Mother and the Sky Gods."

"Yes, er, I mean no!" Antonio replied quickly. "What I mean, Noki, is there may be some things the same with your beliefs, but God is the true God, Jesus is His Son and they are not the same as the gods you know."

Noki looked puzzled. "I do not understand. If some things are same…."

Noki had learned a surprising amount of Spanish in so short a time, but if he only knew it fluently, Antonio thought. *If only I knew more of Noki's language.* He was here to teach the Indians, not try to be like them, he argued in his mind. *But how can I teach them if they can't understand the basic words of my teachings?*

"Ah, Father cannot explain everything," Noki said, not waiting for Antonio to answer. "That is same, too."

Antonio was impressed by the young man's insights. "Yes, Noki, some things between us are the same. Some things I don't have the words to tell you." He got on his knees to wash his face. He used the sleeve of his habit to wipe his face "Noki, if you come to the lessons, you might understand more about God and Jesus."

"Maybe, sometime." Noki cupped his hands to drink.

The boy stood ready to continue down the path. Antonio remained on his knees and prayed. When they resumed their journey, Antonio continued, "Noki, I do save people. I help them get to Heaven. What you call the Starry Path."

Noki's eyes lit in understanding. "It was good you came to Eti."

At the place where he had slipped and fallen, Antonio located his staff near the edge of the path. He rubbed his thumb against the smooth wood and felt grateful to have found it. This staff had helped him walk along many paths in Spain, Mexico and Alta California.

They came within sight of the mission about mid-morning. Someone shouted to the others working nearby. Within a few minutes there was a small crowd gathered around him. When he reached the main building, he noticed Noki was no longer by his side. He saw the boy heading up the path towards the hills and his village. "Noki!" Antonio called out, and when the boy turned back to him, "Vaya con Dios!"

Noki waved, and ran up the path. Soon, he was out of sight. Father José greeted Antonio. "I was beginning to worry about you, Father."

"I was fine. It was too late to come back last night," Antonio explained. "Noki was kind enough to come with me and make sure I made it back safely."

"Was your undertaking a success?" Father Jose asked.

"Yes, and no. The boy died, but I was able to give him the last rites. I now see how I can bring these people into the fold of the Holy Mother Church. I will explain over a bite of breakfast," Antonio said, walking into the building toward his small bedroom.

As he ran back to the village, Noki thought about Eti. No more would his younger brother be at his elbow asking questions, watching his every move. No more laughter, no chatter, no high-voiced cries of triumph when Eti had caught a rabbit in a snare or hit a gopher with an arrow. He was so proud of his hunting prowess when he provided dinner for the family. Suddenly, despite his best efforts, Noki began to cry. Part of him was ashamed of his tears, but he could not help it, he missed his brother so much. He felt sick to his stomach and had to swallow several times to avoid throwing up. Taking a deep breath, Noki looked up toward the azure sky.

He went over in his mind everything that had happened—things he could have changed; things he might have done wrong. Had he angered the gods? He had not stopped Eti from going to the white men. But others followed the white men and hadn't died. He remembered Maria. She followed the white men's gods. The white men's gods, his gods—who was truly listening?

He went to a nearby streamlet, and washed his face and his body. He wanted to be as clean as he could be for the cremation of his brother. With his quick bath finished, Noki ran back up the trail.

When he trotted into the village, Noki sensed something wrong. He hurried to his house where he found Aunt Sachac rocking back and forth, crying. Eti's body still lay on the ground, washed, as was customary, his winter clothes and other belongings by his side. Eti's hair was oiled with the fat of a groundhog and tied back with otter fur. His face was decorated with paint to show the sky gods one of the people was coming to travel the sky path.

Eti should be in the ceremonial house, awaiting the time when his body would be placed on the pyre that would be lit at nightfall. It was a necessary part of the ceremony allowing him onto the Starry Path, but here was the body still in their home. Eti appeared asleep and Noki had an urge to shake his brother awake. Noki looked to his aunt for answers.

"Your father, mother and Chaht are in the canyon finding a suitable place for Eti's cremation and the burial of his bones," Sachac said, her voice trailing away to another song of sorrow.

"Why is he not in the wamkish being attended to by the elders?"

"For the same reason Kawawish would not attend Eti while he was sick."

So Kawawish's pronouncement extended beyond death. "Who is going to lead the ceremonies?" The implication of the situation sank in. The village priests saw to all the ceremonies and rituals. In something as important as death, it had to be done right or the gods would be angry.

So who was going to make sure Eti's spirit went on its way to the Starry Path? Now worry crept into his heart. Eti had unbalanced things, at least that was what Kawawish had said. Did that mean Eti deserved to wander in spirit in the village unable to join the ancestors? *Of course not!*

'*I can bury him in the mission cemetery,*' Father Antonio said. He had also said the God Jesus was on the Starry Path waiting for Eti. If that was so—if the white priest could oversee the death ceremonies….

Noki remembered Koowut telling him how the white priest had withstood Kawawish's power. Father Antonio was powerful enough to send Eti to the Starry Path.

If Noki took Eti's body to the mission, Father Antonio would care for him and make sure everything was done right so Eti's spirit would he happy.

"I will go tend to your sister and leave you to watch your brother," Aunt Sachac said.

He was unable to believe his fortune. Some god was helping him! After she left, Noki took his pouch from its peg on the wall. Into it he placed his ceremonial skirt and some of Eti's personal things.

Noki tied the mats around Eti so his brother would be enveloped in a tule cocoon. Noki slid his arms under his brother's body and left. Outside, he saw several women nearby. The soft wailing stopped until he had walked by.

In the place where his parents would pass on their way back home he met Aunt Sachac.

"What are you doing?" she asked.

"I am taking Eti to one who has the power to send him on the Starry Path."

"The Sosabitom who came last night?"

"Yes," Noki replied.

"But he is a white man," his aunt reminded him.

"He has as much power as Kawawish has. Perhaps more."

"Kawawish warned us about the white men," Sachac protested. "Eti didn't listen."

"You don't understand why Eti did what he did," he retorted. His anger deflated. "I'm sorry, Aunt Sachac. I didn't mean to sound so angry. Eti felt friendship from the white priest. He felt power in their gods to take away any affliction. He thought the white priest could take away his . . . his...."

"Stuttering?" Sachac asked softly. "Did that mean so much to him?"

"I told him it didn't matter, but it did to him. Some of the boys teased him."

"You truly believe this white priest can speak to the Ancestors and the gods to allow Eti on the Starry Path?" she asked.

"I know that our priest will not!"

"Your father will be unhappy."

"I know, Aunt Sachac," Noki replied. He felt his decision weighing down on him as though a rockslide had swallowed him up.

Sachac sighed, the sound in her throat like the rustling of butterfly wings. "I will wait for your parents at the mouth of the canyon and tell them what you have said."

"Thank you." Hopefully Father would come to see Eti on his way to the Starry Path.

"When all the gods are satisfied, come back home, Noki."

"I will."

Sachac touched his cheek and lightly caressed the mat-covered body in his arms.

Turning in the direction of the lowering sun, Noki began the long and difficult journey.

Chapter Eleven

Noki walked the same path to the mission he had the day before with such desperate hope. Each bush, each tree, everything reminded him of journeys he and Eti had made to the Sosabitom village. *Why had they come?* Eti had been drawn to them, as other local villagers had. *But why Eti?* Father had said things were changing, but why did they have to change? Why couldn't things stay the same?

A rock slid under his foot and Noki brought his mind back to the path before him. He felt the ground with his foot before putting his weight down. Insects buzzed around his head and sweat dripped down his neck.

By the time the sun reached the shoulders of the western hills, he could see the mission in the distance. Noki heard a bell ringing several times and he quickened his pace, remembering what Juanito had told him about the messages of the bells. He didn't want to miss Father Antonio if the bells were signaling the time to sleep.

To his dismay, there was no one in sight when Noki approached the river. He feared it might be too late in the day for Father Antonio to accept his brother. He trod carefully across the cold and slippery rocks.

Noki came to the building where he had found the priest the night before. He checked the priest's room, but no one was there. He heard singing and decided to follow the voices to their source. Noki came to a large room in the adobe building where many people were kneeling with heads bowed. Above him, the golden light of sunset slanted through a network of poles laying in a loose pattern from one wall to the other. At the far end of the room, Father Antonio and another priest were chanting something Noki did not understand. He moved closer to the priests. The people kneeling on the hard dirt floor gaped at him, their eyes large in astonishment.

The priests were shocked into silence, but Father Antonio acted first. "You brought your brother," Father Antonio said. Noki was not able to speak. "You are very tired, my son. Let me take Eti." He let the priest take Eti from his leaden arms.

"Father José, would you finish the vespers?" Father Antonio asked as he left the building. Noki followed, not knowing what else to do.

Father Antonio took Eti into a smaller room and laid him on a raised wooden structure. With gentle care, the priest pulled away the mat from Eti's face and used his fingers to comb his younger brother's hair, which had become disheveled in the journey. Father Antonio walked over to another wooden structure, one that was something like the drying racks in his village, and making the white man's god sign across his chest, pulled out a long white stick from a holder in the wood. Noki noticed other sticks lit like little torches, their flames flickering as though they were dancing. Eti had described these and called them 'candles.' Father Antonio's held one end of his candle over a lit one and soon it was burning, too. He placed the candle back into its receptacle and turned to Noki.

"Your entrance caused quite a stir in Vespers," Father Antonio said, punctuating his words with signs.

Noki was not sure but he thought the priest was angry with him. "I'm sorry. I did not know. Is God Jesus angry now?"

"No, he isn't. But why did you bring Eti here?"

Noki had to pantomime much of his explanation. "Kawawish not do the . . . ceremonies to let Eti join ancestors in spirit world. Kawawish said Eti belongs to other gods now. Old gods would be angry if Kawawish did ceremonies. You are priest of gods Eti followed. Please send Eti on the Starry Path," he begged.

Father Antonio said nothing. Noki wondered if despite his previous words, the priest was angry he had brought his brother to him. "Of course, I will perform Eti's burial, but where are your mother and father?"

Noki hung his head, feeling the guilt at not telling them.

"Your mother and father didn't come with you?"

"They . . . they not know," Noki stammered. He began using his hands to convey his words. "They were going to burn Eti and bury his bones without the words and songs to send him to the Starry Path."

Flies buzzed around Eti's head. Noki reached over and closed the mat. Eti needed to be cremated soon.

"You believed he wouldn't find heaven . . . the Starry Path, without someone like me or Kawawish to send him there?" Father Antonio asked, his voice low and gentle.

"Yes."

Your parents should be here," the priest said.

"Aunt Sachac said she was going to tell them."

"Do you think they will come when they know?"

"Yes."

"I will send someone to watch for them, while we prepare your brother," Father Antonio told him. "You need to rest for a few minutes and wash up before the burial."

"Please, let me stay here and watch over Eti." Suddenly, Noki couldn't stand to be away from his brother. He had to keep the flies away.

As though reading his mind, Father Antonio pulled the mat tighter around Eti's head. "Eti will be all right. This is a special room. You rest."

Noki *was* tired. "For a short time." He looked around the room, watched the candles flicker, their little flames reminding him of what soon must be done. "Where will you burn his body?"

The priest looked puzzled for a brief moment, then his eyes widened as though some new thought came to his mind. "Is that what your people do with the dead?"

"Of course," Noki said. "You are a priest, don't you do that with your dead?"

"No, we bury them in the ground and say the right things that will let the dead go to the Starry Path."

Noki was momentarily taken aback. "How can Eti go on the Starry Path if he is not burned?"

Father Antonio took a breath. "Because that is the way God wants it. I promise you; Eti **will** find his way to the Starry Path."

Noki believed the Sosabitom priest.

In the background the music continued, swelling and then getting softer. Strange though it sounded, it was soothing to Noki's ears.

Two men came into the room. One was Noki's age, the other older. "Father José sent us to help you," the older man said.

"Thank you, Juan," Father Antonio said. He gave instructions that seemed to be more like the buzzing of bees than words. Noki felt an instant of dizziness before it passed. "Are you all right, Noki?" the priest asked, gazing at him in concern.

"Yes," Noki replied. Father Antonio didn't look like he believed him, but it didn't matter.

The priest laid his hand on Noki's shoulder. "Juan will take you to the men's house where he will help you get ready for the burial."

"Come with me, Noki," Juan said in the language of the Payomkawichum. "You need something to eat." Juan led him out of the building and toward a house built more in the manner of his people. This one, however, was larger, made with heavier poles. Noki paused a moment before entering.

74

"It is safe," Juan told him.

"A ceremonial house is not this big," he said, looking upward toward the large hole that let the smoke from a central fire escape. "Why so large?"

"Most of the men of the mission sleep here," Juan explained. "There are almost thirty of us. We need much more room than a regular house would give us."

"Oh."

"Come, let me find you clothes to wear," the man said.

"I have brought clothes to be worn at the death ceremonies," Noki declared. "I need no others."

"But you do. The decorated skirt is not enough. The Fathers would like us to be properly clothed for all things we do here."

"I will wear the clothes of my people," Noki insisted, reaching into the pouch at his side and pulling out a tule and feather skirt. He shook it out carefully, making sure that all the feathers had come through the journey without harm.

"It is beautiful," Juan said appreciatively, touching the feathers that fringed the bottom. "I hope you will be able to wear it. Father Antonio is not so strict about these things as some of the other priests are."

Noki only wanted to finish what he needed to do and get back to Eti. "I must go to the stream and wash."

Juan led Noki to a small pool partially hidden by reeds. "That is where the men bathe in the evening."

Noki stepped into the water. First, he poured water over his head, intoning prayers of supplication to the gods to make him a worthy witness to the ceremonies to come. He poured water down his back and over his chest. Noki scooped up a handful of sand and used it to scrub his body. When he was finished, he waded out of the stream. Juan handed him a shirt, much like the one the older man was wearing.

"I must wear this?" Noki asked, feeling the rough material.

"Yes, out of respect for the Fathers."

With Juan's help, Noki put on the shirt. It itched and it was all he could do to keep from tearing it off.

"Come, we will finish finding you clothes."

"I am still wearing my skirt," Noki declared.

"I think Father Antonio will not mind that," Juan said as they walked back to the house.

"Good," Noki replied. When he returned to the men's house, he reached into his pouch and pulled out a baleen comb. The water had helped loosen some of the snarls, but it took longer than he wished to make his hair presentable. When he was satisfied he tied it back with the strip of leather.

"By the way, Noki, I forgot to welcome you to the Mission San Luis Rey," Juan said.

"I will be here long enough to do the mourning ceremonies for Eti and for the gods to soften their anger toward my family...." Noki began, but couldn't finish. His words stuck in his throat. He had taken Eti without his father's permission and he realized he might not be going home.

"What is it, Noki?" Juan asked. "It's about your brother and your family, isn't it?"

"Yes," Noki whispered. He wished his parents were here, so he could smell the earth and wood smoke scent of their bodies, feel the warmth of their arms and the gentle sounds of their voices.

"Teresa is sending you dinner," Juan said, laying a hand on the boy's arm. "From what Father Antonio told me, you have not eaten for over a day."

"I am not hungry," Noki said, shaking his head.

Juan didn't move. "I had a son once. He was three-years-old when he died. It was very hard."

Noki glanced at Juan a moment, seeing sadness in the older man's eyes. He remembered when Eti was three. He had brought a fox kit to the village. Father allowed him the companionship of the animal until it nipped him. Kawawish told them it was against the will of the animal gods to keep something like that in the village. Father took it away and let it go where he knew other foxes had dens. Eti grieved for the kit for several days.

Noki related the story to Juan.

"It is good to remember someone who has died," Juan said soothingly.

"But the djudjamish ceremony is supposed to make you forget the person who has died!"

"I know, Noki," Juan replied. "I don't believe we are to forget the person we loved, but only the pain of his passing. Right now you feel sadness, you may even feel guilt that you did something that caused your brother's death. But that sadness and guilt will someday go away, and you will remember your brother with happiness. Even as I remember my beloved Esal."

Noki had never thought of the djudjamish mourning ceremony quite like that. He was comforted by the older man's words. They sat without talking, listening to the sounds of the early evening—the frogs by the river, the mourning doves and owls, and crickets.

"I will see what happened to your food. Pahe probably ate what Teresa sent for you," Juan said with a slight smile.

"I am not hungry. I want to make sure Eti is buried first."

"Very well, Noki. Perhaps we should go to the capilla and see if Father Antonio is ready to bury your brother."

"Capilla?"

"It is the place where you left your brother," Juan explained.

Noki put on his skirt, making sure the feathers hung straight. He looked up at Juan. "I forgot the paint to put designs on my face for the ceremonies."

"That is all right. At a Sosabitom burial we do not paint our faces," Juan assured him as he pulled back the doorway covering for Noki.

The sky had darkened a great deal, but Noki was able to see figures coming down the hillside meadow from the east. *Father and Mother?*

Chapter Twelve

Father Antonio stood near the boy's body, surrounded by myriads of candles. He pondered the import of the events of the past twenty-four hours and prayed for understanding and direction. After a few minutes, he turned his attention to Eti. His parents had carefully prepared him for burial. The body was clothed in a skirt and a fur cloak. His oiled hair was tied back. The scent of aromatic oil warred with the smell of death.

Father José entered the small room. "Would you like me to dress the boy for burial?" he asked.

"No, his parents already have. Manuel needs to get several neophytes and dig the grave."

"I will tell him and be right back," Father José said.

Antonio watched the flickering candles, studying the flame of the one he had lit for Eti. He remembered his visit with Eti and his mother. It had been right after the dedication of the new mission. Eti had been eager to learn. He remembered the boy telling him that Jesus was like the Indians' sun god. He had been so excited at the similarities.

"Juan is bringing in the older brother," Father José reported. "He also said the dead boy's parents are here.

Antonio started. He had not heard the priest's approach. "Good. I will greet them." Walking out into the twilight, Antonio could barely make out the small group. He walked a short distance and stopped to wait. Soft footfalls from behind told him Noki and Juan had joined him. Father José stood by his side, a candle in a sconce lighting the area immediately around them.

Noki's father, mother and another man stopped in front of him. They all stood in awkward silence.

"I bid you welcome here," Antonio said. Juan translated.

"My heart is filled with grief and anger, but this is not the time for anger," Kwalah said.

"You are right, this is a time to think of Eti and the journey he must make."

"I was told you have the power from the gods to send my son to the Starry Path."

"Yes."

78

"Let me see my son," Kwalah said.

"Of course, and while you are with Eti, I will make sure everything is ready." Antonio wondered at the wisdom of leaving these people alone with the body. He could come back and Eti might be gone. On the other hand, he felt Noki and his parents should have some time alone. Antonio led the group into the capilla. "I will return soon."

In his room Antonio prayed again. He pulled out his alb and amice from the chest where he kept all his vestments. He placed the amice on his head and adjusted it, pulling the hood of his habit over it. The white linen alb slipped over his habit, and he secured it with a special linen cincture. After Antonio made sure he had everything he needed, he genuflected one more time and left.

When the Sosabitom priest showed the group into the small candle-lit room, Father, Mother, and Uncle Chaht stood in awestruck silence for several minutes. Noki watched as his father walked to the table where Eti lay and pulled back the mat that covered the boy's face. All three had on their ceremonial skirts and mother had accentuated the small tattoos on her chin and wrists with paint. Father and Chaht had oiled and tied their hair back with strips of otter fur. Mother began to sing. The candles flickered in the deepening darkness, as though dancing in time to her voice.

Juan entered the room. "I will carry the boy to the cemetery," he said.

Father shook his head. "I will take my son to the place of his burning."

"Here the bodies are not burned, they are buried in the ceremonies that will more quickly send them to the Starry Path and the Ancestors," Juan explained.

Father stared at Juan, frowning before turning to Noki. "Did you know this?" Father demanded.

"No, Father, I only knew Father Antonio had power from his gods to send Eti to the Starry Path." He gulped in a breath of air.

Father gazed at the body lying on the table, at Noki and at Tahmahwit.

Mother laid a hand on his arm. "Hasn't our child been shunned enough? Here he has been accepted, even if the ceremonies are different. Let him be buried here so that his spirit can join the ancestors. We can sing the tuvish and other ceremonies later, in a place of your choosing."

"My sister speaks wisely," Chaht concurred. "Whether it was right or wrong for Noki to bring Eti here, he is here and the Sosabitom priest is willing to do the ceremony."

Father seemed to deflate like an empty water skin. "Very well, let him be buried in the Sosabitom manner. But I will carry him to this place of burial and I will lay him into the ground."

Without warning, an apparition of white seemed to float in from the darkness. The priest looked ghostly in his white clothing, and his silence made the similarity to an ethereal being more complete. Only when he greeted them did Noki's family relax.

Father handed a soapstone pipe to the priest. "This is a gift."

"Thank you," Father Antonio said. "I am honored by your gift."

"My son," Kwalah said, pointing toward the dead boy.

"Yes." The priest hesitated a moment, as though trying to fathom what Noki's father was thinking. "I will bury him now and send him to the Starry Path—to heaven."

"Yes, bury. We sing songs." Kwalah picked up Eti.

Father Antonio led the way from the room. When they reached the place of burial, Noki saw there was a hole dug to receive his brother. He swallowed hard. It all seemed so final. There were several torches nearby to give light and by them he could see the sorrowful faces of his family.

Father José motioned for Father to lay Eti down beside the grave.

"No, if he were in the village, I would be laying him on the pyre. I will hold him until the priest speaks to his gods and they say it is time to bury Eti."

Father Antonio stepped to Kwalah's side and made his god's sign in the air over Eti's body. "It is all right," he said. "You hold your son during the ceremony." He began the words of the burial, allowing Juan to translate.

Noki tried to concentrate on the words, but it was very difficult. The figures around him seemed to flicker like the dancing flames of the torches.

The priest finished and made the god's sign again. "I am sorry Eti died," he said. "He was a good child; inquisitive and friendly. I will miss him." No one else said anything. Father Antonio motioned for the body to be placed in the pit.

Kwalah placed Eti into his burial place. Mother began singing, a sound somewhere between a moan and a wailing that Noki felt echoing deep in his heart. As Father pulled his arms from beneath Eti's body, he reached into a pouch at his side and removed several items. There was Eti's hunting net and snare. There were several arrowheads Father had made recently and there was Eti's throwing stick. Mother put in a small woven basket with some of Eti's possessions.

Father stepped back and began singing. Mother lowered her voice in deference while Kwalah sang the song of farewell. When he finished, he stared at the mat-wrapped form in the dark hole.

Noki stepped forward and pulled off his necklace. His thumb felt the smooth edges of the stone Eti had found on the beach. Eti had worked on the stone, drilling a hole in it through which he had strung a leather thong. Noki laid the necklace on top of the other gifts.

"Come with me and we will let the others finish burying Eti," Father Antonio said to Father when they had finished leaving their gifts.

"No, I will wait." Kwalah stood fixed, his arms by his side, his fingers flexing as though they could not be still. The priest motioned to Juan and Manuel to cover the body. Noki cringed. While he knew Eti was journeying to the ancestors, each shovel full of dirt seemed to tear a piece from his heart.

When the task was finished, Father said, "We will return to our village now. We thank you for asking your gods to take Eti."

"You are welcome, Kwalah."

Now Father turned to Noki. "I understand why you did this thing, but it will take me a while for the hurt and disappointment to leave my heart. Your mother and sister and I will be traveling to the village of my relatives. I would like you to live with your Uncle Chaht and Aunt Sachac for a season."

Noki felt his head pounding with the pain of too many emotions.

"You are still my son," Father said. "We can talk during the acorn gathering season."

Tahmahwit gave him a loving hug and they left, swallowed up in the darkness.

Chaht waited until they were gone and touched Noki's shoulder. "Come, we will travel home together."

Noki tried to speak, but his breath caught in his throat and all that came out was a sobbing sort of sound. What should he do? He didn't want to go back to the village and watch his parents leave without him. On the other hand, he didn't want to stay here where things were so strange. Uncle Chaht solved the problem for him.

"You appear tired, Noki. Maybe it would be better if you slept here and return tomorrow," he suggested.

Noki appreciated his uncle's astuteness. "Yes, I am tired."

"We will be waiting for you. Take as long as you need."

"You go with Juan and sleep. After Mass tomorrow morning, we can talk," Father Antonio told him.

Noki barely remembered the walk to the men's house, and didn't remember lying down at all.

During the night the dreams began. They were more vivid than any he had ever had before. He was on a beach, preparing to launch a raft to hunt seals. The waves were gentle and he pushed the boat out into the water. All of a sudden, one wave rose up higher and higher, curling like an old man's hand before it crashed down on him, swallowing him up and then spitting him back out onto the surface of the ocean.

Noki shook the water out of his eyes, astonished that he was still in the boat. He paddled, frightened by what had happened, but determined to get meat for his family. He continued to paddle as the sun beat down. In an instant the sun stopped shining and Noki looked up, wondering why the sky was so dark. Clouds boiled overhead, bounding like deer across dry and dusty meadows. He had never seen clouds like that and they alarmed him more than the wave had.

The sky darkened until Noki couldn't see the boat he was sitting in. Suddenly, a fish of enormous proportions leaped out of the water. Its eyes were large and luminous, bright like the sun. The mouth was huge, a dark cave ready to engulf him. The fish leaped once and dove back into the sea. It broke the surface again, rising higher and higher into the air, water dripping from sparkling scales. Noki picked up a spear sitting next to his feet. Cocking his arm back, he made ready to attack. He tensed, trying to put all of his strength into the throw. Noki flung the spear at the monster fish. It sped unerring toward the gaping cavern of the fish's mouth and disappeared.

Noki knew it had struck the great sea beast, because the fish thrashed from side to side even as it hurtled toward him. The mouth gaped wider and wider. Snatching a knife, Noki tried to prepare for the impending attack, but he knew it was useless. The fish opened its mouth and engulfed him. He was surrounded by total darkness. Noki screamed, but his voice echoed back to his ears and hurt them. He struck out with the knife, but found nothing.

"You cannot fight me," a voice thundered in the darkness.

Noki's heart pounded in his ears and he felt a heat as though he was in a fire. He was afraid, but didn't know what he could do to save himself.

"Noki," a small voice called to him. It was almost a whisper, but Noki recognized it instantly.

"Eti?" he asked. "ETI?" Hope filled the places in his heart where despair had lodged. His brother was alive! "Where are you?"

"I am in your heart, Noki."

"In my heart?"

"Yes, brother. Remember me and I will always be with you," Eti said.

"You are not alive?" Noki asked, disappointed.

"Yes, I am alive in your heart," Eti answered. "No matter what path you choose, I will be with you. Never forget me."

"You are on your way to the Starry Path? Truly?"

"Yes. I thank you for bringing me here and letting me go to the ancestors."

"I would do anything for you, Eti!"

"Listen to your heart and follow its path," Eti said. His voice was getting whispery and remote.

"Eti?"

"I must go now. There are those gathered, waiting...."

"Waiting for what?" Noki asked. There was no answer. "Eti?" Again, there was no answer. "Eti?"

"Noki," another voice said to him. It was an older voice, deep, but it sounded kind.

When he opened his eyes, he saw nothing. Noki was afraid he was still in the huge monster fish. He thrashed out with his arms and one hand was caught in a firm grip.

"Noki," the voice repeated. "It is all right."

As his eyes adjusted to the pre-dawn darkness, Noki recognized Juan. "I . . . I had a dream."

"What was it?"

Noki sat up and related the dream, leaving out nothing. He felt drained and weak.

"Ah, it was a good dream."

"He told me to always remember him and he would be with me."

"Very good!"

"He said he was on the Starry Path to meet the ancestors, and then he was gone and you were here."

"Eti will be with you as he promised. He will be like the angels the Fathers say guard and help us," Juan said.

"Angels?"

"Good spirits, like those the Sun God sometimes used to send to people he liked."

Noki slowly got to his feet. He felt light-headed and dizzy, but it passed in a moment. He put out his hand to steady himself and missed the wall, falling to his knees. His stomach wanted to rebel, but there was nothing to get rid of. Noki heard voices, but he couldn't understand them. He felt the same darkness he had experienced when he was in the belly of the fish and Noki remembered no more.

Chapter Thirteen

"Padre! Padre!" a young voice interrupted Antonio's pre-Mass meditation.

"What is it, Paku?"

"Juan told me to tell you Noki is sick," she said in a rush.

He hurried to the men's house. The boy was burning with fever. "Take him to the hospital building, Juan. Have Anna watch over him until I return."

"It's the same illness his brother had," Juan stated.

"Undoubtedly, but with prayers and good care, he will recover," Antonio replied, hoping it would be true.

As Antonio prepared for Mass, he heard a soft sigh. Paku stood in the doorway. "Yes, my child?"

"Mamá wanted to know if you would like her to use Spanish medicines for Noki, or could she to use her own medicines."

They hadn't received many medicines from San Diego yet. "Your mother has her own medicines?"

"Sí, Padre, she brought them when we came to the mission," the five-year-old explained.

"Tell your mother to use her own medicines," Antonio said.

The girl dashed out of the room, her feet stirring up clouds of dust as she pattered away.

Antonio would have to talk to Anna about her medicines. If they worked, he wanted to know more about them.

After Mass, he went to see Noki. The newly constructed infirmary was small, perhaps four or five sick people could fit inside with their attendant. Thankfully, Noki was the only patient.

Anna was coaxing him to drink something with an interesting aroma. Noki drank all of the medicine without fully waking.

Antonio kneeled down beside the boy and touched his forehead. The fever was high. "What remedies are you using?"

"Padre, prayer is the best remedy," she replied. "These sicknesses take many, leave some. My little girl did not die, her father did."

85

"I know, Anna," he said. "Noki's name was added to the prayers list. But I am also interested in the medicines that you are using to help the sick. What did you just give Noki?"

"It is *huvamel* and it helps fevers. The crushed seeds of the *qaashil*, or what you call sage, make a good wash for sore eyes.

"You are going to have to show me these plants you use. Gather and store any herbs that can be used for the sick," Antonio instructed her.

Noki began coughing. Anna took a damp cloth and wiped the boy's face with it. "Paku, go get fresh water."

"Yes, Mamá."

Antonio knew Noki was in good hands and left to organize the day's work. He studied his designs and drawings. The future buildings formed in his dreams as well as on the paper. Antonio began his progress report to the Father Presidente. He finished the letter and examined his supplies, listing what the mission needed.

He went out to the enramada, where he saw a carved stone laid at the head of the Eti's grave. Someone had placed flowers on it.

Children were already gathered for instruction. He began with a song about the birth of the Savior, pantomiming various parts. Antonio kneeled in the dust to draw letters. The children took turns copying the marks. As they sang another song, a small boy climbed up on his lap. A thumb was in his mouth, his other hand played with Antonio's rosary.

"Come," he said when he finished. "Let's go check the pumpkins." The small but enthusiastic group led Antonio to the garden.

At lunchtime, the priest visited Noki. This time there was a mat over the door to protect Noki's eyes. "How is he?"

"The fever is still high, Padre. The cough is no worse. He woke up for a short while, very thirsty and took most of the broth Theresa sent. I believe he will recover."

Noki woke up and almost panicked when he couldn't open his eyes. He started to rub, but someone caught his hand. His head pounded and his throat was dry. When he coughed his chest hurt.

"Drink this," a woman said. "It will make you feel better. In a little while I will clean your eyes."

"Where am I?"

86

"You are at the mission."

"Who are you?"

"I am Anna. Now drink this."

He did, feeling the roughness in his throat ease. "Thank you."

"I want you to take this other medicine. It won't taste as good," she said. "But it will help the cough go away."

She was right; this drink was foul tasting. Noki didn't argue, trusting that Anna knew what she was doing. *Do I have the same thing as Eti?* His family would not know when he died. "Will Father Antonio send me on the Starry Path when I die?"

There was a pause before Anna answered. "Noki, I think the Virgin Mother has intervened for you this time. You will get well," Anna said.

"Why would she do that? I don't believe in the white man's gods."

Anna laughed as she washed his face. Noki thought her laughter was very soothing, like the flowing of a stream over the rocks.

"Are you sure about that? You brought your brother here for the burial," she countered.

"I wanted the priest to send Eti on the Starry Path."

"The Virgin Maria will intercede for all who need her. Many people here have been praying for you to get well, none more than Father Antonio," Anna said as she gently wiped his matted eyes.

"Why didn't she help Eti?" Even after Father Antonio's explanation, he still wondered.

Anna shrugged. "There are different reasons for death. Sometimes people are allowed to live for a special reason. Father Antonio told us the story of one of the Saints...."

"Saint?"

"Someone special, who has done things so good he is allowed to go right to God after he dies," Anna explained.

Noki yawned, tired beyond measure. "What did this saint do?"

"He gave away all his things; his house, his clothes. He went around helping those who were sick and poor," Anna said. "It was what God wanted him to do. His name was Francis. Father Antonio is one of his helpers," she went on. "He came all the way across the ocean to teach us about God and to show us a better way to live."

Noki said nothing. He wondered how he could live any better than he had in the hills with his family. Of course, now there was no Eti.

The next time Noki opened his eyes, he saw Father Antonio sitting beside him. The priest was drawing on a flat piece of wood that lay on his lap. There was a basket by his feet. When he picked up a plant to study it, he noticed Noki watching him.

"Ah, you are awake," Father Antonio said. "Would you like something to eat or drink?"

"Drink, please."

After Noki had his fill, he sat up. "Anna said you pray for me," Noki said. "Why? I am not baptized."

"I pray for everyone," Father Antonio replied.

"How long I sick?"

"Five and a half days."

"Anna says you come to teach how to live better. Why? My people live as we want."

Father Antonio hesitated a moment. "I am here because God wants me here."

"What does Spanish God want here?"

"Noki, I love God. I want to do whatever He wants me to do," he said. "God wants me to teach everyone about his Son, Jesus."

"Some do not want your gods," Noki said.

"It is because they do not understand them."

"Maybe." Noki stifled a yawn. He needed to finish asking his questions. "Why your god make my people leave homes?"

"What?"

"Kawawish say Spanish priests make my people . . . stay in the missions." Noki struggled for the right words. "Not able to leave."

"Noki, the people are here at this mission because they want to be. I do not make them stay here if they want to leave. Don't you remember? I let your brother and Mother go."

"If I want to leave when well?"

"I'd be sad, but I wouldn't make you stay. I wouldn't want you to if it made you unhappy."

Noki knew the priest was telling him the truth. With that reassurance, he drifted back off to sleep.

Chapter Fourteen

Noki sat at the edge of the river, watching the sun set, the rays shimmering in the last of the afternoon heat. It had been three weeks since Eti was buried and Noki was completely well. Today, he had helped Manuel lay split boards across the church building, although he wished he were making arrowheads instead.

Noki felt it was time to go home, but always something kept him here for another day. He had helped Juan build an addition on the men's house, helped Tahvah harvest corn, worked with Father Antonio identifying plants. It was nothing anyone was doing deliberately. Noki couldn't seem to find the proper time to leave. He shook his head. Time? He was slipping into the mission train of thought. He was getting used to the bell that rang for Mass, the work periods and everything else.

In the village, things were done when they were needed. Hunting was done when there was game in the area. The acorns were harvested when they were ready. New houses were erected when the village moved.

Noki watched several of the younger children pulling weeds from the pumpkin patch. These pumpkins were larger than similar fruits he found wild in the hills. When he had been recruited to help harvest the first corn, Noki had been amazed at how much was gathered. He thought it was much more than needed, even for the coming months.

One of his companions, Miguel, had tried to explain the need for so much. Noki just shook his head in confusion.

"I do know this," Miguel said. "Father Antonio has worked hard to keep us alive. We have food and we have homes."

Noki couldn't dispute the fact that Father Antonio worked hard. Last night Noki had gone to Father Antonio's workroom to teach him some of the customs of his people. He received no answer when he tapped on the doorframe. He called out softly, but there was still no answer. Noki assumed Father Antonio was helping someone who was sick. He was about to leave, but he heard the soft sound of someone sleeping. He peeked into the dimly lit room. Father Antonio was sitting at his worktable, papers scattered all over its surface, pen and inkbottle in one corner. The priest's head rested on one arm and he was sound asleep.

Noki stared for a moment. In the time he had been at the mission, the boy didn't recall seeing the priest rest much. He was always teaching, planning, or supervising the construction. Noki realized Father Antonio did care about him and his people, at least in his own way. He pulled the woolen blanket off the cot in the corner and laid it across the priest's shoulders. Noki turned to leave,

"Noki…." Father Antonio said sleepily.

"I'm sorry I woke you, Father," Noki responded.

"No, we were supposed to study tonight."

"Sleep is important, too."

"Yes, it is, but there are so many things to do," Father Antonio said with a yawn. "Hmm, let us work for a bit. Then I will follow your advice." He motioned Noki over to the table. They discussed Payomkawichum customs and language until they were both yawning in fatigue.

Noki realized he needed to leave now or he would never leave. He liked the feeling of belonging to this group and he was comfortable around Father Antonio. There was something about the priest's religion that attracted him, too.

The sky had softened to a dark reddish-gold twilight. The bell sounded for vespers and it would soon be time for dinner. "So you come out to say good-bye to the sun also," a voice said.

It was Tomás, a Payomkawichum a few years older than him. Tomás occasionally slipped away during the day, coming back at dinnertime. "I came out to think," Noki said.

"About leaving?"

"How did you know?" Noki asked.

"My father was the shaman in his tribe," Tomás said. "I know things. I also know that you have not yet been baptized."

Noki laughed. "One wouldn't have to be a shaman's son to know that. Gossip travels like water in the river."

"You will never leave here," Tomás stated, ignoring Noki's joke.

Noki bristled. Of course he was going to leave. He had a family back in the village. At least he had Uncle Chaht and Aunt Sachac. He would be able to go with them at the acorn harvest to see his family. "I will be going home soon. I am well now."

"You were well a week ago," retorted Tomás.

"I know. There is a part of me that likes it very much here, but I belong with my people."

"I have the same feelings."

"Why don't you leave?" Noki asked.

"There is no family to go to," Tomás said sadly. "They are all dead."

"Sickness?"

Some of them." Tomás didn't elaborate.

"Do you believe what the priests teach?"

"Yes, well...most of it. I think the Spanish gods are more powerful than our gods."

"How so?"

"The Spanish are eating up the land, making our people go where they don't want to," Tomás said. "If Chinigchinich was stronger than these new gods, our people would not have sickened and died. They would not need the help of the Spanish priests or their gods. Our men could have fought against those evil Sosabitom—and sent them away from our lands!" He paused and looked out at the deepening twilight. "But Chinigchinich is weak, or old, or . . . dead." His voice was almost a whisper.

The thought startled Noki. "Dead?"

"Is that so foreign? Other gods have died. Remember Ouiot? And Jesus died, but he was powerful enough to come back to life. I think the Spanish gods killed our old gods."

"But why couldn't . . . can't all the gods get along?"

"Think about it. What happens in the lodges where two families are living together?"

Noki bit his lip to keep from laughing. Yes, he had heard some of the bickering in the night and the gossip by the streams in the mornings.

"Even the gods fought among themselves at times," Tomás said.

"The only gods left are the gods of the Spanish?"

"Don't you think so?" Tomás asked.

"I don't know. All I know is that I miss my family."

"I miss my family, too," Tomás replied, his voice melancholy. "I try to do the right things now so I can be worthy to join them someday." He paused and they both listened as the insects whirred, clicked and buzzed. "I know I'm not as good as Father Antonio would like me to be. But as much as he tries, he does not understand our ways."

"He would like to baptize me now."

"It's important to him. He doesn't think we'll find the Starry Path if we're not."

"But I can't do that, even for Father Antonio, until I can truly follow his gods," he said.

Tomás took a deep breath. "Enough of this sad and hard talk. We do the best we can, Noki, and let the gods decide if we have been good or bad."

They walked to the mission church without saying anything, each engrossed in his own thoughts.

Later that evening, Noki tapped on Father Antonio's door.

"Ah, Noki, we are not scheduled...." Father Antonio stopped when he saw the look on the young man's face. "What is it, my son?"

Somehow Noki felt as if he was betraying this man who had shown him kindness. It didn't matter that they sometimes didn't understand each other. Father Antonio still liked him.

"You want to go home...."

"Yes."

"You worry about your family, don't you?"

"Yes, Father, I do," Noki said. "I am thankful for what you have done for me and Eti. You are like a father to me." He blushed. His last sentence sounded silly. Father Antonio was called father by everyone at the mission.

Father Antonio's blue eyes crinkled into pleased understanding. "I thank you for the compliment. A father cares for his children, always wanting the best for them. I want the best for you, Noki."

"I know, Padre."

"The mission is always open to you. I will also be visiting your village soon."

"I can help talk to the villagers for you." Noki felt better.

Father Antonio laughed. "Oh, yes, your Spanish is much better than my Tamancus."

Noki hid a smile behind his hand at the priest's understatement.

"I will miss you, Noki. I will miss our talks."

"I will miss you, too, Father Antonio." Noki waited for the inevitable question. "You are not going to ask me to be baptized before I leave?"

"No. You will join the Mother Church when you are ready."

There was an awkward, silent moment. "I will leave first thing in the morning."

"Let me give you a blessing now," the priest offered.

Noki kneeled and listened while Father Antonio prayed over him. When he ended with 'Father, Son and Holy Ghost', Noki felt peace in his decision.

Father Antonio embraced him. "There are special things for you to do, Noki. Remember what you learned here."

Noki decided not to wait until morning. In the men's house, he pulled off his trousers and shirt.

"Father Antonio would expect you to take your clothes with you," Juan said.

"Are you sure?" he asked. "I have nothing to trade for them."

"You have helped at the mission," Juan replied. "That is all that is asked."

"Nevertheless, please give this to Father Antonio," he said, pulling off the leather thong that he wore around his neck. It had a stone he had chipped into the form of a cross. Noki made it to remind him of Eti, but he didn't need a stone to remember his brother. He would rather the stone help Father Antonio remember both of them.

"I will, Noki," Juan said. "You are really leaving?"

"Yes. Tonight."

"I will miss you," the older man said. He studied Noki's necklace in the soft golden light of the fire. "You have learned the stone knapper's art."

"Yes, my father was the weapon maker for our village," Noki replied, pleased that Juan recognized his skill.

"You are to be his successor?"

"I don't know. It's up to the leaders and the new weapon maker."

"You have the skill to be a weapon maker now, without someone over you."

"Thank you, Juan. I hope I can still make the arrowheads."

"I am sure you can," Juan pointed out.

Noki laid his hand on the older man's arm. "You have helped me much and I am grateful."

"You are welcome, Noki. Don't forget to visit sometimes," Juan reminded him.

"I won't. Father Antonio said he was coming to visit soon, too."

"I'll come with him. I would like to see your village," Juan said. As with Father Antonio, there was an awkward silence. "May the Holy God be with you."

"And with you, too, Juan," Noki replied. He pulled the pants back on, but put the shirt into his pouch.

"Here is something for your journey, Noki," Juan said, pressing a small, leaf-wrapped package into his hands. Noki could see it was flatbread. There was an ear of roasted corn as well. "Thank you, Juan." He slipped out into the moonlit night. It was a half moon and not as bright, but Noki's feet were sure and he was soon across the river and jogging toward the hills, toward his village. What he would find, Noki didn't know. All he knew was that he was going home.

Chapter Fifteen

Father Antonio double-checked everything he was taking for his journey to Noki's village. In one pouch Theresa had packed enough to eat for several days. Anna had given him several envelopes of herbs, including his favorite, huvamel. It would make a wonderful tea for the cool nights.

The other one contained everything he needed for teaching the Indians; holy water, crucifixes and newly made necklaces to give as gifts. There were also dried seeds of corn and pumpkin to show how such things could be cultivated.

Slinging the pouches over his shoulders, Antonio put on his hat and picked up his walking stick. He went to the almost finished kitchen building. It was open on two sides, to allow breezes to keep the area cool, with a branch and sloping mat roof to protect the earthen ovens and fire pits from the sporadic rains. It would be impossible to finish everything Antonio wanted done before the winter season set in, but much had been accomplished. A plank roof was on the Church now, and the new, more permanent buildings for the men and women's living quarters were in various stages of completion.

Most of the local Indians had joined the Holy Mother Church. Some of them were living at the mission, but many remained in their rancherias. Vineyards had been planted nearby with cuttings brought from San Diego. A rancheria to the west was being prepared for wheat and corn production. A small amount of wheat had been planted, while the rest would wait for spring.

Now Antonio was going into the hills to teach. Although it had been two weeks, he missed Noki and looked forward to seeing him and teaching in his village.

"Is there enough food in your pouch, Father?" Theresa asked. She was an older Indian woman who had arrived at the mission with her brother, daughter and grandson shortly after its dedication. "I can pack more for you if there isn't."

"Yes, more than enough, thank you. You are spoiling me."

"I want you to have what you need for your journey," she told him. "I will have beef and steamed clams when you return."

"Theresa, I will be as fat as those cows out there if you keep this up," he said with a chuckle.

Theresa snorted. "I do not think so, Father. You eat a little and then you are out walking around the mission, going to the rancherias."

"Stop worrying, Theresa. I am fine. You take care of me as well as my own mother would."

Her eyes showed pleasure at his compliment. "That is a good thing. It is bad when a son is far away from home. When you see your mother again, tell her I took care of you."

"When I write my mother I will be sure to let her know how much you have cared for me," he said, touched by her concern.

Juan joined him, carrying the bedrolls along with a pouch of food. The bells for breakfast sounded as Antonio and Juan crossed the river. It was a clear day, promising to be warm, but comfortable. Birds twittered from the tops of nearby trees and the grass crackled under his feet. The way was pleasant and Antonio felt they would get to the little rancheria by noontime.

Noki sat atop the ridge of the canyon near the village looking for promising rocks for spear points. The amount of stones he had found was light compared to what he should have gathered by now. None of the stones felt right. Noki didn't think it was the rocks, but his own lack of focus. He often thought of the mission and the friends he had made there.

When he had arrived home, his aunt and uncle greeted him with cries of joy. It was almost sunrise before he finished his story.

Noki was comfortable with life in the village, but there were moments of inactivity when his hands wanted to do something, or when his feet wanted to walk out to a field that didn't exist here. There was also the rosary. Father Antonio had given it to him when he was sick, and Noki continued to keep it safe in his pouch. Some days when he was looking for arrowheads stones, he rubbed the beads and talked to Eti. Sometimes he imagined Eti answering him, but Noki figured it was just the breeze whispering in the brush.

Soon they would be going further into the hills for the acorn harvest. Kawawish had consulted his sacred objects and declared they would go in two moon cycles.

"Your mind seems very far from the stones." Uncle Chaht sat beside him. "You changed while you were away."

Noki knew that, and it bothered him. Uncle Chaht was right. He didn't know who he was anymore or what was right. Was Kawawish right? Or was Father Antonio? He asked his uncle.

Chaht took a deep breath. "I don't know if one is entirely right and one is wrong, Noki," he said. "I think it is the fact that the two cannot live together."

"Why not?" Noki asked.

"If you were grown and married, would you want me and your aunt living with you?"

"A friend at the mission said something like that. But there are times when families have lived together and gotten along without any trouble," Noki pointed out.

"True. Perhaps the two ways of living do not get along because men don't want to learn different things. Each priest thinks he walks the only right path, but maybe neither man is altogether right or wrong on how to best approach the gods. It is confusing."

They sat in silence for a long time, watching an eagle float overhead, oblivious to its surroundings. Noki envied the bird.

"I was angry at Kawawish, too," Chaht said after the long silence. "But I decided there is nothing to gain by hating him. I still have my family. I am still Payomkawichum, living the way of the people. I am afraid of the white people, but I'm glad their priest was willing to help Eti onto the Starry Path."

Noki wondered why his uncle would be afraid, but he remembered his own confusion and understood.

"I was worried about you. Especially when you didn't come home after a few days. I thought the white priest had taken you away from us. Your parents were worried, too."

Mother and Father? "They knew?"

"Yes, Noki. Some time ago, a young man came from our cousin's village. Mainly he was here to give a message from his captain to ours about the upcoming acorn harvest, but the messenger also visited me. Your father inquired about you, if you were back from the Sosabitom village and if you were all right."

Noki felt relief at the revelation. He wondered if, in some ways, Father Antonio *had* taken him away. "I don't know what path I will take. I wanted to come home the whole time I was sick, but I didn't want to leave the mission, either."

"That is the way with men. It seems there is something inside that makes them restless, always wanting something more."

"I didn't want more before the white men came," Noki protested.

"Weren't you eager for your manhood rites so you could be a man?"

"Well, yes, but...."

"Ever is it so. One is a child and he wishes to be grown. One is grown and he wish for youth, or more children, or whatever he doesn't have," Chaht said the last as much to himself as to Noki. His uncle and Sachac had not been blessed with children.

"Sometimes that longing for more, or for something different is a good thing, Noki. Do not disdain that which pulls you toward it, at least until you know if it is good for you or not."

"How will I know if it's good, Uncle?"

"You have to listen with your heart, Noki," Chaht said as he got up to leave.

Noki remained in the same spot overlooking the village, thinking over his uncle's words. He gave up trying to listen to his heart and watched the landscape below. After several moments, he thought he saw figures coming up the path through the far end of the meadow. There were two figures, a man covered in gray material and another man of the people. Father Antonio!! The priest had kept his promise; he had come to the village. Juan was with him, too!

Noki continued to watch, not moving from his perch. He was excited, but he wanted to see how Father Antonio and his people greeted each other.

A mother looked up and called her child to her. Other women waited cautiously as Father Antonio strode toward them, greeting them cheerfully. One of the women was Aunt Sachac. No one moved toward the pair of visitors, but neither did they pull away. Noki was thankful there was no breeze that would carry the voices away from him. He could hear the conversation clearly.

"Miiyuyam!" Father Antonio called out. "I am Father Antonio Peyri. I am here to visit and to give gifts," Father Antonio added.

Aunt Sachac approached Father Antonio. When she was standing in front of him, she looked into his intense blue eyes. "I thank you for helping my nephew, Eti, go on your Starry Path," she said.

Juan leaned forward and spoke to Father Antonio, telling him what his aunt had said.

Father Antonio said, "You're welcome. You are...?"

"I am Sachac, Noki and Eti's aunt."

"Bless you, my child," he said, making the sign of the cross over her. Next Father Antonio reached into a large pouch at his side. He pulled out something Noki recognized as the corn cakes the women made in the mission. "Since it is time for the midday meal, here is a gift for you and the others," he said, handing one to Sachac. She took it hesitantly but did nothing with it. Father Antonio broke up another one and took a bite of it. "It's good to eat," he explained.

Sachac took a bite of the food. Apparently, she enjoyed it because she took another. "It is good," she said.

Father Antonio broke up the rest of the cakes and gave everyone a piece. He pulled out a roasted ear of corn and gave it to Sachac. "This is what these cakes originally came from," he said while she examined the corn.

"You can eat this, too?" she asked.

"Yes," Father Antonio replied.

She took one bite and then another. Noki remembered how much he had liked corn the first time he had tried it.

Father Antonio explained how the corn cakes were made from the corn. Someone asked where she could find this new food and Father Antonio pulled out his dried seeds. Planting crops was unheard of among his people. The priest pantomimed plowing, planting and harvesting the corn. Everyone watched silently. One of the children picked up a stick and imitated the priest, scraping a furrow in the dry earth.

Father Antonio placed several of the seeds into the freshly dug soil and covered them up. The people began bombarding him with questions. That was when Noki saw Kawawish and several men striding out of the village. He scrambled to his feet and dashed down the trail.

Chapter Sixteen

Antonio was encouraged by his ability to communicate with these villagers with minimal help from Juan. He heard the approach of other villagers and saw that it was a group of men, Kawawish in the front. Antonio didn't relish a confrontation, but he felt calm inside and ready for anything.

"Why do you come?" the shaman demanded.

"To visit."

"There is nothing we need from white men," Kawawish growled. "Go back where you came from."

"Why are you afraid of me?"

"White men killed many of his people long ago," another voice said in Spanish. It was Noki.

Although happy to see the boy, he restrained his greeting. The import of what Noki said sank in. The shaman had more than the loss of power as a reason to hate him.

"Speak the language of the people and not the tongue twisting of these Sosabitom!" Kawawish snapped.

"I know both languages," Noki said. "I can act as translator for you, for Captain Oomaqat and for Father Antonio."

"We do not need to talk to him," Kawawish said. His hands made motions of great disdain.

"He comes in peace," Noki said. "He buried my brother when you would not and he took care of me when I was sick."

"He turned you away from our people and our gods and made you his slave," Kawawish retorted.

Antonio watched the exchange quietly, trusting Noki.

"I am here, Kawawish. I am not at the mission. Father Antonio and I talked many words, but I was allowed to leave anytime I wished.

Kawawish eyes snapped with anger. "You are not part of his religion?"

"No. He teaches, he asks, but I have not said yes . . . yet."

"White men bring death; they kill the old ways."

"Maybe that is true, but there are some new ways that are good," Noki said, his voice conciliatory. "Why can't the people hear what Father Antonio has to say and then they can decide."

"That is all I want," Antonio said. "I wish to show you ways to grow new foods, and to teach what I believe is good."

"We have acorns, we have deer," one of the men retorted. "There are seeds, roots and berries."

"But what about times when there are no acorns, seeds or berries? What happens when the rabbits and deer are scarce?" Antonio countered. "This was grown this summer. Taste it and see that I have brought a good food," he said, pulling another ear of corn out of his pouch.

Kawawish knocked the corn out of his hand.

Antonio felt a quick nudge of irritation, but he squelched it. He knelt in the soft soil and touched the corn.

"There is an old story about seeds," he began. He reached into his pouch and pulled out more of the corn. "Jesus, the Son of God told the story of a man who planted seeds. He prepared his field for them...."

"The seeds we gather do not have to be planted," one of the onlookers interjected. "The wind plants, the birds plant."

"This man wanted many seeds to grow for his family so there would be food during the cold and wet times. He wanted seeds and meal to trade for other things he needed," Antonio explained and then waited while Juan translated. "The man's field was ready and he went through it, sowing the seeds." He stood and pantomimed the motions. Everyone watched, curious. "Some of the seeds went among the rocks."

"It is hard for plants to grow in rocks," a woman said.

"Exactly," Antonio said with a smile. "Birds came and ate some of the seeds. Some sprouted but because there was no place for the roots to grow, the plants died in the hot sun. Some of the seeds fell among thorny briars and weeds." This time no one interrupted him. They were waiting to hear more.

His hands moved almost rhythmically, pantomiming and enhancing the story. Antonio continued telling the parable of the sower. "But some of the seeds fell to the good soil and they sprouted."

"Enough!" Kawawish bellowed. The shaman leaped toward Antonio, brandishing his club.

Juan and Noki jumped in front of Antonio.

"No!" Oomaqat shouted. Kawawish practically skidded to a stop, his countenance darker than a thundercloud. Captain Oomaqat stood resolute and

Kawawish lowered his arm. "I wish to listen to this man's stories," he said. "Those who want to hear can join me. Those who do not want to listen can go elsewhere. As leader of this village that is my decision."

"To listen is death," Kawawish said.

Oomaqat simply folded his arms over his chest. "I do not see this one trying to take us as slaves, as you have said. If he tries, **I** will kill him," he stated.

"I will curse him to die so he does not make you slaves with his words," Kawawish spat.

"That is your right," Oomaqat said.

Kawawish stalked toward the ceremonial hut.

Antonio thanked Oomaqat in the people's language. He took off his large brimmed hat to wipe his sweaty brow. Several people gasped at his bright red hair.

"Finish your story," Oomaqat said, unaffected by the priest's appearance.

Antonio put his hat back on, pleased that he had gained at least minimal acceptance from the leader. "Of course, Captain," he said. "The seeds sprouted, and grew tall and strong in the good soil. The plants grew large as they ripened. Finally the fruit was ready. The man who planted the seeds came out to his field and cut the plants down. He brought them to a special place where food is stored. He had so much that it could not hold it all. The many seeds that came from each plant were enough to feed himself, his family and all who wished to trade with him."

"All of this from a handful of seeds?" a girl asked.

"Yes, if the seeds are planted in a good place, and they are cared for, the harvest can be great." He pulled out his last ear of corn. "This came from one seed and there are always two of these on the same stalk."

"It is like the oak trees that grow from a single acorn," Noki added. "But this grows more quickly."

Antonio handed the roasted ear to Captain Oomaqat. "It is not warm, but it's still good," he coaxed.

Oomaqat looked at it, but would not eat. "You eat," he said.

Antonio complied. He handed the corn back to Oomaqat who took a small bite and chewed carefully, as though ready to spit it out.

"It has a good taste," Oomaqat said.

"Yes," Antonio said.

"And it makes the flat cakes you gave the women?" Oomaqat asked.

"Yes, it does," Antonio replied.

Oomaqat asked other questions about planting and using the corn and Antonio answered them all. Finally the captain turned to Noki. "You are not a man yet, but I will ask you a question and I want you to answer me as a man would answer."

"Of course," Noki responded solemnly.

"Do you trust this man?"

"I would trust Father Antonio with my life. His heart is good. He took care of me when I was sick and cared for me like I was his son."

"You will stay in my house tonight as my guest, and tell more stories," Oomaqat told Antonio. "You will not try to ensnare my people with your words, or I will do as I said before. I will kill you."

Even though Antonio understood much of what Oomaqat had said, he let Noki translate for him, just to be sure.

"I have never ensnared anyone, Captain," Father Antonio said. "I speak the truth, even in my stories. I want to help those I visit. If they believe my words, I am happy. If they do not, I am sad, but I will do nothing to harm anyone." He pointed to the corn in the captain's hand. "The truth I speak is like the seeds that produced the corn you hold in your hand."

Oomaqat looked puzzled.

"Some of my words, like seeds that fall upon rocky ground, are heard, but not taken into the heart. When something happens that makes the listener doubt, like the harsh sun on the seeds in rocky soil, the word withers. Or sometimes the words are plucked away by those who fear the words, like the birds do the seeds that fall along the wayside. But those who take the words into their hearts are like the seeds in fertile soil. You hear my words and let them grow in your heart and you can decide if they are worth keeping or not."

Oomaqat pondered Antonio's words. "You speak well. I will listen to you tonight. Tomorrow, you will show me more of this thing you do with seeds. Then I will decide if what you say is of worth or not."

"I appreciate your hospitality, Captain," Father Antonio said, bowing his head in respect of the Indian leader.

While the priest was in the village, Noki stayed by Father Antonio's side. Noki didn't need to be in the shaman's house to know he was conjuring curses against the white priest. He made sand paintings outside his house. He spent hours in the sweat lodge. At night, Kawawish sang and chanted, often loudly and very late.

When his curses didn't work after the first day, Noki noticed Kawawish spying on the white priest. Sometimes the shaman would try to get close, but when he saw Noki or Juan watching, he would mutter and stalk away. Father Antonio told Noki he was being overcautious, but the boy continued to carry all of the priest's things he didn't carry himself. Noki knew if Kawawish could get a hold of something belonging to the white priest, the curse would be more powerful. If Father Antonio died Kawawish's authority would be great in the eyes of the people.

Noki also kept an eye on the preparation of the food served to Father Antonio. He made sure Captain Oomaqat's wife or Aunt Sachac were the only ones who cooked Father Antonio's food.

"If he did get something of mine, the power of God would prevent Kawawish's evil curses from working," Father Antonio reassured Noki.

Noki saw this as another instance of the white priest not understanding the ways of the people. "Maybe so, but I do not wish to let you take a chance. And if he could get close enough to take something of yours, he could also put something in your food to make you sick."

"You have a point there."

"I will keep watch," Noki asserted. He felt his cheeks grow hot. It was not his place to order one older than himself.

"You are a brave young man," Father Antonio reassured him. "I'm happy you are my friend."

At the end of the third day, during dinner in Oomaqat's house, Father Antonio announced his intention of leaving for the mission the next morning. "I hope I have not been a burden," he told the captain.

"No, you have told many fine stories," Oomaqat said. "I hope you will continue to learn our language so we can exchange stories next time you come to visit."

Noki noticed the sparkle of pleasure in Father Antonio's eyes. The priest had hoped he would be invited back to the village.

"Thank you for your hospitality. I have enjoyed staying with your family." Father Antonio stifled a yawn. "I hope you don't mind me going to sleep early. It is a long walk back to the mission."

"I wish to think about what you have said, perhaps talk with your companion," Oomaqat said. Without waiting for an answer, he left, beckoning Juan to join him. Noki was curious, but didn't follow, as he had not been invited. He sat staring at the doorway.

"Noki, I will be fine," Father Antonio said from behind him. "Go on home and I will see you in the morning."

Noki slipped to a shadowed area by Oomaqat's house and sat listening the group of men.

Oomaqat sat by the fire that crackled and popped with newly added branches. Noki saw Uncle Chaht sitting there, along with several other men of the village. To no one in particular, Oomaqat said, "I know the white priest wants us to accept his gods. I want to know your thoughts, but first, I want to ask you, Juan, why you have accepted these new gods."

"At first I accepted them because I had to."

"Explain," Oomaqat said.

"I lived in a village many days journey to the south. When I was a young man, the Sosabitom came to our village with soldiers and a few priests. They told us we had to accept their gods or we would die. Some of our men fought these soldiers, but the white men were stronger and had powerful weapons. When their weapons were fired, it was like the rumbling the ground made when the old gods were angry. We were frightened so we stopped fighting. We let the Sosabitom priests put the water over our heads. They made us leave our village and live in their mission further south. We did things that seemed strange at the time and the priests in their village taught us to speak their language and follow their gods."

"Why didn't you escape?" Kwila, the under captain, asked.

"The soldiers with their guns were too powerful. We prayed to our gods and we were answered with sickness and death. Most of my people died, including my mother and father."

The men muttered amongst themselves. There had been sickness in the village seasons before. It had been a time of fear.

"Those of us who were left did the things they wanted us to do." Juan shrugged. "We did not have a choice." Noki wondered with all that had happened to him, why Juan could be so happy.

"There are no soldiers here," Kwila said, his voice angry. "We can kill this priest and you will be free."

"No!" Juan cried out, then lowered his voice. "You cannot do that."

"You show great loyalty to this white priest, despite what you have told us," Oomaqat countered.

"There are two kinds of white men," Juan said. "Many of them have hearts of stone and are cold and arrogant, thinking they are gods themselves. I used to think they were all like that."

"But now?" Uncle Chaht prompted.

"First of all, let me tell you that no amount of cursing will ever kill or send away the white men," Juan said. "I have seen their big villages. The one called San Diego is like a hundred of your villages put together. They will continue to come and finally cover the land. There is nothing we can do to stop them."

"Do you pretend to see the future?" another man asked in derision.

Juan laughed. "I'm no priest, but I know what I have seen."

"Why are you so loyal to this priest?" Uncle Chaht asked.

Noki thought it a fair question.

"Because there are a few of the white men whose hearts are good. I met one in the mission in San Diego," Juan said. "He treated me as though I was a man and not an unruly child. I understood that in his own way, he cared for us."

"But one out of all those in that huge village?" Oomaqat asked, incredulous.

"There are some others," Juan replied.

"Why did you come to this white man village?" the captain asked.

"Father Miguel thought I would like it here. I wanted to be away from all the soldiers and their guns. I wanted to see the hills and mountains again."

"And this priest?" Kwila asked.

"He, too, does not know what lies deep in our hearts, but he cares," Juan said. "He is different. He does not want to force the people to live at the white man village."

"And his gods?"

"They are not so far from the old gods. The Holy Mother Maria is like the Earth Mother, nurturing and giving. The God Jesus is like Ouiot."

"Ouiot became wicked," Chaht pointed out.

"In that way they are different," Juan countered. "God the Father is like Chinigchinich, who is over all."

"I will think on your words, Juan," Oomaqat said in dismissal.

Juan ducked into the captain's house without acknowledging Noki. The boy continued to listen.

Almost as one, the men sighed, but said nothing for several minutes. "He is not the first to say such things," Oomaqat said.

"Then you don't think there is any chance Kawawish can force the white men away?" Kwila said.

"No," Oomaqat said. "I believe Juan. Father Antonio is one of those few white men with hearts of something other than stone."

"What do we do?" Sula asked.

"I need to think about this, my friends. I don't want our village to be swallowed up like Juan's," Oomaqat said.

Chapter Seventeen

Everyone stared into the flames of the fire as though it would give them the answers they needed or wanted. Noki slipped away to think about what he had heard. Despite the fact that he had heard all of the men's concerns before, he was still confused.

"You are very deep in contemplation to not hear me," Uncle Chaht startled him a short while later.

"I don't understand. How can one people have two different hearts?" Noki asked.

Uncle Chaht sat down next to him. "You know that even our people vary in the content of their hearts. I have been with this white priest. I have listened to him, seen how he treats the children. I see a good heart."

"I know, but Juan and Kawawish were not speaking falsely," Noki said.

Chaht laid his hand on Noki's arm. "I don't have to be a shaman to see these are hard times."

"Did the captain decide anything?" Noki asked.

"Oomaqat decided we should be friends with the Sosabitom priest. He left the decision of how friendly to each individual," Uncle Chaht replied.

"What do you mean 'how friendly'?"

"Only that if the people want to accept the white man's gods, they can do so. If they don't want to, that is all right, just as long as they don't harm him."

"What about Chinigchinich and the old gods?" Noki asked.

"Noki, I don't know. My soul is empty of answers right now."

"Tomás says they are dead. Do you think the new gods warred against Chinigchinich and beat him?"

Chaht shrugged. "I believe Juan when he says the Sosabitom will never leave. We must do the best we can to live with them and not anger them into sending their soldiers against us."

Noki was appalled. "Do you think Father Antonio would allow that to happen?"

"No, but he is not the captain of all the Sosabitom."

"Do you believe what Father Antonio has said?" Noki asked, knowing his uncle had been to most of the teaching sessions in the past two days. "About his gods?"

"I see truth in many of the Spanish priest's words. The words about caring for each other are similar to what the elders teach." Uncle Chaht paused a moment. "I see that your heart is drawn to this priest for some purpose, although you resist letting him 'bap-tize' you. Why is that, Noki?"

Until he had talked to Father, Noki would not allow himself to be baptized. "I have to be sure," was all he said.

"That is good. Do not change the way you feel," Chaht said.

"It's hard, Uncle. I'm glad to be home, but...."

"Go back with him," Chaht advised.

Noki looked at his uncle in shock. Go back? He shook his head. "Father named me his assistant. There is no one to make the new arrowheads."

"Noki, I don't think your future is in making arrowheads." When Noki said nothing, his uncle continued. "Father Antonio is a good man. Perhaps your place is in helping this white man understand our people a little better."

"Who will make the arrowheads?" Noki protested. "What about Father and Mother? I want to meet with them during the acorn gathering. I want to see them again...."

Chaht shook his head. "Your father left all of his finished arrowheads in my care." His uncle laid his hand on Noki's shoulder. "As to your family . . . when the acorns are ready, come back and go with us. Your father will be ready to talk by then."

He felt relief at Uncle Chaht's words. "Thank you."

"Didn't you tell Kawawish that Father Antonio would let you go as you willed? Go with the priest tomorrow. If your heart someday leads you back here, you will still have a place among us."

The next day, Noki watched as some of the people in his village were baptized. Most of them were children, but some were adults like his uncle and aunt, Kwila and his wife, and Oomaqat, the captain. After the baptisms, Father Antonio celebrated a short Mass. Juan had carried a bottle of sacramental wine and a loaf of bread up the mountain, and Father Antonio gave a portion to each person who had been baptized. The rest of the villagers looked on. For once, Kawawish could not be heard chanting.

Noki sat by the stream waiting for the priest to leave. He had his belongings with him.

A short while later Father Antonio came down the path. "Thank you for helping me, Noki. It would have been much harder without your assistance."

"I wish to go with you."

The priest looked surprised. "I thought you wanted to stay here, Noki."

"I can still come with you, can't I?"

"Yes, of course you can! You are always welcome at the mission."

"You will need someone to help you in other villages. Juan won't be able to go with you all the time."

"Yes, I daresay you are right," he said, his eyes showing his pleasure. "I've missed you, Noki."

As they crossed the meadow, Father Antonio sang a song in Latin. When they started down the first gully, Noki felt a prickling at the back of his neck. He looked around in alarm. Something was out there!

Antonio thought about the last three days' events as he, Noki and Juan traveled along the familiar path. He felt buoyed by his success at Oomaqat's village. To have eight children and five adults baptized in this village was greater than he had expected. Antonio wished Noki had been baptized with the rest. Then a new thought occurred to him. Noki would be an asset to the work here, not because he was a member of the Holy Mother Church, but because of what was inside him. Noki's uniqueness would strengthen those around him, including himself.

A sharp cry echoed through the air. At the same instant, a lithe body flew at him. All he could see were the yellowed teeth of his attacker, the red, black and yellow paint that circled glaring and hate-filled eyes, and a monstrous club in an upraised hand. It looked like something from the depths of Hell, but Antonio knew it was Kawawish. "Holy Mother of God!"

Kawawish swung his club. Without thought, Antonio's fingers curled around the cross at the end of his rosary and he smashed his fist into Kawawish's face, while deflecting the shaman's blow. His knuckles connected with the softer tissues of the Indian's nose. Kawawish howled in pain, blood spurting from his broken nose.

Juan jerked Kawawish back by his hair. With an animal growl, the shaman leaped around and struck Juan with his club, knocking him to the ground, unconscious.

Antonio scrambled to his feet. Kawawish rushed toward him, again swinging the monstrous club. The priest ducked the blow, but felt the wind of its passing. With his fist still curled around the crucifix, Antonio struck Kawawish in the stomach. The old man doubled up and fell to the ground, gasping. Noki grabbed the club and brandished it.

"Noki, no!" Antonio shouted and turned toward Juan, worried about the unconscious Indian.

Kawawish seemed to have demonic reserves of energy. He knocked Noki to the ground, and sprang for the priest's throat. Antonio's knee buckled beneath him with searing pain. The shaman's fingers were talons curling around his neck, closing off his windpipe. It was as though Antonio was fighting against Satan himself and the priest redoubled his efforts. Again, he punched Kawawish, all the while asking for strength to get away from this evil minion of hell. The arm of the crucifix cut into the shaman's cheek. Antonio clutched at Kawawish's arms as the thin, but steel-hard fingers squeezed tighter. He pulled at the Indian's wrists, but it was as if something had welded Kawawish's fingers to his throat.

Antonio felt his heart pounding in his ears. Fear was taking the place of intelligent thinking. Noki yelled something, but it was like a whisper. Antonio tried to pull the hands away from his throat, tried to punch the Indian in the face, but there was no strength in his blows. Then a thought came into his mind. It was the vaguest of whispers, but it made itself heard above the fear and the sound of his racing heart. Antonio saw a picture in his mind and he followed what he was seeing. He put his arms up between Kawawish's arms and pushed outward, his hands balled into fists for more force. It was all one motion, quickly executed. To his surprise, the shaman's grip broke. Antonio followed with another blow to the nose, and another to the chin. Kawawish stumbled away and fell to the ground, his hands covering his battered face. He lay panting in the dirt, moaning in pain.

Antonio stood up, ignoring his pain. Noki held a knobby stick above the shaman's head. The decorated club lay on the ground several feet away. Antonio stared at the fallen shaman in shock and fear. Never had he been attacked in such a manner. Antonio felt his hands trembling and he rubbed them down the side of his habit. He reached over and touched Noki on the shoulder. "No, my son. There is no need."

Noki was breathing hard. Antonio realized how difficult it had been for this youth to threaten the shaman who had been his leader for all of his life. "Noki. It's over." Before waiting to see if Noki responded, Antonio limped over to Juan and checked his injury. There was a lump on the side of the Indian's head, but very little blood. "Juan," Antonio said, checking for other injuries. "Juan," he said more loudly.

Antonio wet his handkerchief from his water pouch and wiped the Indian's face.

Juan groaned and opened his eyes. "Padre, you are all right?"

"Yes, I'm fine. How about you?"

"My head hurts, but that is all."

"Thanks be to God," Antonio murmured.

"You must destroy his club," Noki said, still guarding the stunned shaman.

"Why?" Antonio asked, helping Juan to his feet.

"Because it is an emblem of his power. If you destroy it, it shows that your power is greater than his," Noki said.

"But Kawawish couldn't kill me. Doesn't that show that God's power is greater?"

"Yes, Father Antonio, but there may be someone watching among the rocks. Seeing you destroy an emblem of Kawawish's power would be told back in the village," Noki explained. "They would know you have the greater power."

Antonio saw the wisdom of Noki's words. "Hand me the club."

Kawawish moaned. "I should have used that on you, white man, instead of trying to take your life with my own fingers," the shaman said. He made no move to get up, but glared at Antonio, his lips peeled back into a snarl. Several teeth were missing, and blood dribbled down his chin.

"Why?" Antonio asked, wanting to understand the intense hatred that Kawawish had for him.

"You are a priest of faraway gods, you are a white man and you do not know why I hate you and your kind?" Kawawish spat out a mouthful of blood. "Your people come. They use their long knives, their deadly sticks and their words to kill. The Sosabitom come and demand our women and kill the men who try to fight back. They come into the villages, acting like gods, and curse the people with death and sickness."

Antonio realized this time Kawawish was not speaking in generalities. "When did this happen?"

Kawawish glared again. Antonio tried hard not to shudder. The hate was palpable.

"When I was young your people came and took my wife. Because she fought against them, they beat her, but still they took her to their houses with the other women. They killed the men who fought against them. Later my wife crawled back to the village. Then the sickness began and my son died. My wife never bore any more children."

Antonio stared speechless at the Indian still sitting on the ground. *The soldiers.* He tolerated the soldiers, because the Crown said they were necessary. What Kawawish related sickened him. "I'm sorry, Kawawish," Antonio said. "For what some of my people have done. I only want to teach. To help."

Kawawish painfully got to his feet. "The old ways were enough. You can help by going away!" Kawawish wiped a hand across his bloody nose. "But I know the Sosabitom will stay. Soon the land will be covered with your people. Soon the hearts of the Payomkawichum who are left will be shriveled and Chinigchinich will be forgotten. My people will forget how to hunt, they will forget how to gather acorns, how to ask the sky and the plants and the animals for help. They will forget how to speak with one another; they will forget their names. They will only know what you have taught them. What will happen to my people when you are gone, Sosabitom?"

"I will live my life here, Kawawish, serving and helping people."

"The future is darkness for my people," Kawawish said, his voice low. "Perhaps my curses will someday come true, priest. Maybe what you desire will become darkness for you, as it has become for me."

"Kawawish, I wish no harm to you or the village."

"Maybe you do not mean it, but it has been done." The old man turned and walked away slow, but resolute. Soon he was gone.

Chapter Eighteen

It was silent; even the birds were quiet. Noki handed the club to Antonio. It was decorated with the feathers of eagles, tied with leather strips. Claws of large animals were embedded in the end. He stared at it.

"Destroy it, Father Antonio," Noki said.

Antonio felt pity for the old man who had been such a determined enemy, but he walked to a nearby boulder. He ignored the sharp pain shooting up his leg from his right knee. Antonio smashed the club down. The wood cracked, the leather broke and when he hit it again, the club split down the middle. Half of it fell away, leaving a spicy scent of cedar in the air. Antonio let the larger half fall from his fingers, now wanting to be done with this sad and dark event.

"You should take part of it as a trophy," Noki told him.

"No, the club is broken. That's enough," Antonio said. He felt drained. "What will happen to Kawawish now?"

"His power is gone," Noki said. "I think he will go back to the village of his wife's relatives."

Antonio said nothing, not sure of his feelings at the moment. *Perhaps when all have heard the saving message of the Savior....*

Juan handed Antonio his staff. "It is true what Noki said. The priest cannot stay where people do not believe in him."

Father Antonio leaned on his staff. "The priests in your villages are considered very powerful, aren't they?"

"Yes, Father," Noki replied. "They can cause a man to die or change the weather. Some claim to change into animals."

"Kawawish claimed to do these things?"

"Yes, last year, he cursed a man living in another village. We heard he died very quickly."

"Hmm, I am sure it was a coincidence."

Noki looked puzzled. "Coincidence? What is that?"

"I mean the sickness and Kawawish's cursing happened at the same time. The cursing didn't cause the sickness. I believe the shamans' power is highly exaggerated, uh, made more of than it really is. I do understand how it would be hard to defy someone like that."

Noki smiled. "Kawawish exaggerated his power."

Antonio returned the smile. "Yes. Exaggerated. He was able to trick your people into believing he could change the weather or turn into an animal. I have noticed how quickly the weather can change at certain times of the year. As to turning into an animal, even you were able to flit into my room like a fox when you came to get me that night."

"That is so," Noki admitted. "You have never said you could do any of those things, but you are more powerful than Kawawish."

"That is because my power comes from God, who is real and is the source of all power. I don't need to change into an animal." Antonio flexed his knee. It was still painful.

Juan had been silent during the conversation. "Can you walk down the mountain, Padre?"

"Yes, Juan, I believe I can do that, although it won't be at the speed we were walking before," Antonio assured the man.

"That is good," Juan and Noki said at the same time.

As he walked the path leading to the mission, it became easier. It helped that Noki and Juan set a slower pace.

At a stream Antonio called a halt. "I think I should clean up." *A good place to pause for prayer, too,* he thought. *There is more to be thankful for now.*

Antonio took off his sandals, pulled his habit halfway up to his knees and walked into the water. It was chilly enough to make him shiver, but after a bit it was soothing. He sat on the bank and examined his knee. It was swollen and warm to the touch. Sensing Juan and Noki's scrutiny, he said, "It will be fine after some rest."

Noki grunted. "When is that, Padre?"

Antonio was taken aback. "Rest? I rest during my meditations and prayers."

"You pray on your knees."

Antonio laughed. The boy was blunt anyway. He liked that. "Not for the next few days, I think," he admitted.

Noki took a milkweed fiber cloth out of his pouch and dipped it in the stream. After he had soaked it, he placed it around Antonio's knee. "You need some salve, like my aunt makes in the village. I did not bring any, but I know this sometimes helps, too."

Antonio's skin crawled at the chill on his inflamed knee, but it did take some of the ache away. After a while the swelling went down. "I'm sure Anna will have some type of salve ready for me."

115

Juan watched, saying nothing for a moment. "Perhaps it would be good to let Father José know you are coming."

"Yes, but don't give too many details. It will worry him too much," Antonio said.

After Juan left, Antonio sat basking in the sunlight, watching the tops of the mountains turn a soft golden color. "This land is much more precious than the richest vein of gold," Antonio mused.

"Gold?" Noki asked, confused. "What is gold?"

"Gold is a metal that money and jewelry are made from," Antonio explained.

"Money? Jewelry?"

Antonio paused. Noki's people had no concept of such things. It was an enviable philosophy. "It is much desired by men."

"Not my people."

"No, it doesn't exist here," Antonio replied. "Some people would give their lives for gold. That is what I was saying. This land is more precious than that."

They sat for a few minutes longer. "Father, we must leave soon or it will be dark before we get to the mission," Noki reminded him.

Antonio didn't answer right away. He was pondering. He had sketched what he felt the mission should be like in some future day, but he knew he could not do it alone. It would be people like this boy next to him who would be the reason it was built and one of the means of building it.

The cool water flowed over his toes. The compress had warmed on his knee and that, too, felt good. Antonio would have enjoyed sitting for several hours, but Noki was right. They needed to get back before nightfall.

Antonio would let Anna work her skills with her salves. After a good night's sleep he could plan for his next excursion. If he could visit a few villages each month he would be able to reach all of the outlying villages within a year.

His reflection showed a bruise under one eye. Blood spattered his habit. He looked as though he had been in a full-scale battle. Antonio was grateful to God for saving his life, but with that gratitude, he felt sadness, as though in victory there was also defeat. Perhaps it was his fatigue. "Well, shall we continue?"

Noki helped Antonio up. The sun had barely set when they reached the mission. Juan and Father José were on the trail, waiting.

A few of the women were finishing their laundry, their children playing nearby. As soon as they saw the pair, they shouted a greeting. Noki helped Antonio across the narrowest part of the river. The women's greetings turned to silence as they took in the condition of the priest. When Antonio stepped onto the bank, children touched his stained habit.

"It is all right. Only a slight mishap on the trail," Antonio reassured them.

"Father Antonio, who did you fight with?" one of the mothers asked.

"A shaman," Noki answered before Antonio could say a thing. "And Father Antonio won."

"God was with me," Antonio replied. "I need to change and rest a bit. I will be fine."

Father José, understanding Antonio's needs, said, "Children, if you would run along to the chapel, I will be there in a moment." The children scampered off and Antonio breathed a sigh of relief. He was more tired than he cared to admit. He wanted to go to his room, say his prayers and go to sleep.

"I should go and get Anna," Noki said.

"I'm fine, Noki. You needn't bother Anna," Antonio assured the young man. "I really am fine."

"Good," was all Noki said before trotting off toward the mission buildings.

Antonio didn't think Noki believed him. Flanked on either side by Juan and Father José, he continued his slow pace, aggravated by the knowledge that his injury would hamper his missionary efforts.

"Juan made it sound like you had fought the devil himself," Father José said.

"It seemed like it." Antonio's knee kept reminding him that he needed to find a place to sit down. "We'll discuss this later in my room. Despite what you see, the visit was fruitful. I baptized over a dozen people this morning, including the leader of the village."

"That is wonderful news, Father! And Noki returned with you." Father José was exuberant. "Now all we need is Anna to use some of her remedies on you."

"All I need right now is a bed and some sleep," Antonio said peevishly. "I'm sorry, my friend. When I have had some sleep, I will be better company."

After Father José left, Juan remained in the room. "What can I do to help you, Padre?" he asked.

"You go on to prayers, too, Juan. I will change and join you in a little while. Afterward, we can both go and see Anna. You got quite a bump on your head." Antonio had every intention of joining everyone in vespers, but when he lay down to rest for a moment, he fell sound asleep.

"Father Antonio, if you keep visiting those villages you will not be able to walk to Mass!" Anna fussed as she rubbed an herbal paste on his swollen knee.

Antonio sat under a tree in the enramada. He was irritated at his forced inactivity. Despite taking extra days between visits to more distant villages, the knee had not gotten better.

"No walking for the next day," Anna went on.

"Are you a physician?" Antonio tried not to sound testy.

"I was a capable healer for my people before I joined the Holy Mother Church," she replied. Anna added in a softer tone, "You are needed here, but you won't be able to stay if you do not take care of this now."

Antonio scowled.

"I did not mean that in a disrespectful way, Father. I speak the truth." She wrapped a steaming new poultice around his knee.

Antonio gasped. "I believe I won't have to worry about my knee anymore. You have scalded it off!"

"I beg you to think on what I have said. I do not wish you to become crippled."

Antonio winced at the word, 'crippled.' "Anna, I don't think it's as bad as that."

"Father, there are springs at San Juan Capistrano. Our people have used them for many years. They can heal your knee," Anna suggested.

Antonio had heard of the mineral waters near the other mission. As much as he hated the idea of putting his plans on hold, that could be the answer to this dilemma. "Do you really think these springs would help my knee?"

"Yes, Father. I am sure of it. You could stay there for a short time and after you are well, return. Father José can teach while you are gone."

"Yes, he could," Antonio said, his voice trailing off. He would have to write to the Father Presidente requesting another priest to take his place. Father Antonio wouldn't expect a newcomer to undertake something so unfamiliar. That meant there would probably be no visits to the villages during his absence. Perhaps this was God's way of telling him the mission building projects needed the most attention right now. When he finished listing all he needed to do, Antonio looked around and found himself alone in the deepening dusk. He limped to his room to compose his letter to the Father Presidente.

"I want to go with you, Father," Noki told him a week later. The Father Presidente's response had not come back yet, but Antonio expected it in a few days.

"I appreciate that, Noki, but I need you to help Father José while I am gone to San Juan Capistrano."

Noki frowned. "Will you be long?"

"I sincerely hope not, my son. There is much to do here."

"I have worried about your injury," Noki said. "I . . . uh, I have prayed that it would go away."

"Thank you, Noki. You cannot imagine how much that means to me."

"I lit a candle for you, too. There are many candles lit in the small room."

Antonio had noticed, but not thought they were lit for him. "I had no idea."

"Of course, Father," Noki replied. "Surely your God is hearing the prayers of those who live here."

Eight days later, Antonio greeted his temporary replacement. Father José Panella was an older man from San Diego. The three priests sat together for most of the next afternoon and evening, going over the activities of the mission.

Father Panella taught the morning classes the next day and Antonio was reassured that all would run smoothly in his absence.

He climbed into the little cart that would take him to San Juan Capistrano. Indian believers gathered at the front of the church and he blessed them. As he did so, his mind envisioned a new, larger edifice with buildings all around and many people going in and out. The trees were tall and elegant, the flowers bright with jewel-like hummingbirds fighting over the sweet nectar.

Antonio blinked away his vision and waved good-bye. The soldier driving tapped the horse's rump with his whip and the little cart creaked away. The children ran alongside until they reached the road leading out of the valley. Antonio waved again and turned toward San Juan Capistrano.

Chapter Nineteen

Noki found the children gathered around the new padre wanting to hear the lessons of the morning. "Father Panella? Father Antonio told me I was to help you in whatever you needed."

"What did you specifically do for Father Antonio," Father Panella asked.

His gray eyes that scrutinized Noki seemed almost translucent. Noki suddenly felt nervous. He didn't know why, but he was. "I went with him to the outer villages, helping him translate."

"You are Noki?"

"Yes, Padre, the son of Kwalah and Tahmahwit."

"Father Antonio told me how helpful you have been to him. He also said you were unbaptized. Is that so?"

Noki's discomfort grew. "Yes, Father Panella."

"And why not, my son?"

"I will be baptized when I am. . . ready."

"Perhaps you should join the children while I teach the lessons," suggested Father Panella.

The voice was kindly enough, but Noki felt the new priest was treating him like a child of Eti's age, rather than someone who was almost a man. "I have heard all the lessons. It is all inside and when my heart is right, I will be baptized," Noki explained, his voice even.

Father Panella frowned. "How long have you been here?"

Noki did some quick thinking. "I believe I have been here for about a moon journey this last time. A month."

"You were here before?" Father Panella noticed the children's restlessness. "Run along to the enramada, children. I will be right there."

"Yes. I was sick...." Noki didn't doubt that Father Antonio had also told the new priest about his brother, but it was not something he was willing to discuss with this stranger.

"Tell me more during the siesta this afternoon," Father Panella said, cutting Noki off. "Perhaps today you can help Father José. I'll decide about anything else in a few days."

"Yes, Padre," Noki said. He joined Father José by the now shrunken river.

"I can use your help today," Father José said. "Father Antonio drew plans to dam the river so we would have more water available during the dry time."

"Dam the river?" Noki asked, unsure what the priest was talking about.

Father José beckoned him closer and unrolled a scroll he had been carrying under his arm. Noki recognized Father Antonio's markings and realized what the priest was talking about. "Ah, you wish to build something to hold the water back. Like the beavers do."

"Exactly, Noki. The head of the dam will be up there," Father José said, pointing to an area that filled with water during a rain. "We can hold the water and let it out any time we need to." Father José's stubby fingers showed what he was talking about on the diagram and Noki followed in rapt attention.

The water would not only form a pond, but it would also feed into the stream where the women washed. Noki caught the priest's excitement. "If the water flows too hard into the lavandería, it will carve out a new path that would ruin the place where the women kneel to wash."

Father José looked astonished. Noki almost laughed. Sometimes he wondered if the white men thought his people knew anything at all.

"You're right, it would, but we are going to build a flat section of adobes where the women can kneel and wash. It will prevent erosion if there is too much water," Father José explained.

"Won't the adobes wash away eventually?"

"If they are baked especially hard, it will be a long time before they do."

Why go to the trouble of making adobes over and over again if there was a better solution, Noki thought. "Would it not be better if you placed flat rocks here for the women rather than adobes?" he asked, remembering the women in the village kneeling on flat stones to wash their children.

"Yes, but it would be difficult to gather enough stones of the right size and lay them out in such a way that they all fit together," Father José explained. "Eventually, I think Father Antonio wanted to lay tiles."

"Tiles?"

"Yes, they are something like adobes, but they are harder and will last longer," the priest said. "In the future, they can be made here."

"So the adobes would be for a little while," Noki mused aloud. He studied the natural stone piled to one side. "These are for the dam?"

121

"Yes."

The form of one of the large stones suggested a face to him, at least part of a face. He saw another stone that could be fitted with it. He could picture where the stone could be chipped and shaped and how the other stone could be fitted with it to make a full face.

Noki had seen Father Antonio's drawings of what he wanted the mission church to look like and remembered the sketches of the statues the priest had drawn. Father Antonio told him they were representations of the Virgin Mother, Jesus, and other special and holy people. Saints, he called them. The statues fascinated him in their detail. It had been hard, at first, for Noki to imagine a stone carver being able to create something that lifelike in stone. He thought the Spanish stone carvers must have a way of seeing into the stones they carved.

Noki wondered if there could be something here by the river similar to what Father Antonio wanted on the church. Noki liked the idea of a god watching over those who came to use the river. If he wasn't able to shape the rocks the way he wanted, he thought, they could be used to make the dam.

"Do you have an idea about this?" Father José asked, breaking into Noki's reverie.

"I think so," he said, but hesitated telling the priest what his thoughts were. He wasn't sure how they would be received. Noki decided not to mention his idea with the stones. "So the water will come from this dam that will be built," he pointed. "To this place and then flow out onto tiles where the women are washing or getting water for the mission."

"That was the way Father Antonio envisioned it." Father José drew in a deep breath and let it out slowly. "I have a harder time seeing what things will look like than Father Antonio. He has envisioned the entire mission finished, from the main church to the granaries and the cattle sheds."

Noki knew what Father José was saying. Father Antonio often talked about things that were in his head or on the paper on which he drew, including statues, paintings and carved designs. Although he was impressed with Father Antonio's drawings, Noki had never attempted anything so large. He would have to work in the evening, or maybe by the light of the moon in order to keep his project a secret. Excitement for his idea built inside his heart. He was determined to make it work.

Noki had brought his chipping tools, but they wouldn't be useful until he had shaped the big stone with the white man's iron tools. He would have to get used to them first.

"For the stairs coming down the hillside, the adobe bricks will be fine," Father José explained, breaking into Noki's thoughts.

Noki half listened while he planned. The youth thought of the other tools he would need.

"Go and gather Gabriel and his brothers, and Tomás. All of you can work together on the dam. "

"Oh, yes, we can do that, Father," Noki said. That he would be working in this area was a wonderful stroke of luck, he thought. Or maybe it was the gods working in his behalf. "I will gather the men and we will begin working here."

"Good! Let's go to the shed and get the tools."

Noki realized the stones he had selected to work on would have to be taken from the pile before work began on the dam. "I will join you soon. I wish to study this for a few more minutes," he said. Noki crossed the river where the piles of rocks lay. He had to pull away a few other rocks, but he managed to pull the stones from the pile. Grunting with effort, Noki lugged them across the shallow river to a spot near a willow tree. There he covered the stones with grasses and sand until he could work on them later. Noki dashed toward the mission where he found Father José handing out tools.

"You have not gathered your workers yet?" The priest's tone was reproachful.

"No, Father," Noki said, still trying to catch his breath. "I was down at the stream, still thinking about Father Antonio's plans for the dam."

"Hmm, it's beginning to get hot," the priest said, gazing up at the sun. "Find men to help smooth the path down to the water so we can lay the first adobes tomorrow."

Later that afternoon, Noki went to the willow-branch tool shed and studied what was available. There was a metal flat-bladed tool that looked a good candidate for shaping stones. There was also a pick. It looked too big for his purpose, and Noki dug around until he found a smaller pick that could be held in one hand. He slid them in his waistband and trotted down to the stream.

Noki studied the stones he had chosen. The sun shone over his shoulder and onto the two rocks, causing them to glow in the late afternoon light. He reached out and touched the larger stone. There was a slight hollow on one side. Noki studied it, trying to see inside the stone; to feel its strengths and weaknesses. It was cool under his fingertips and the power of the ages flowed from its heart to his own. Excitement filled him and Noki felt the rightness of what he was doing. It was almost like the time he made a perfect arrowhead, before . . . before everything had changed.

There was a temporary pang of loss but it was replaced with quiet calmness. This sculpture would be a gift for Eti as well as for Father Antonio.

With the pick, hammer and chisel, Noki practiced smoothing and shaping what he determined to be the back of the stone, until he got a feel for working with these strange, but wonderful tools. Only then did he begin working on the part where the eyes would be. With small, easy strokes, he formed the eyes. They were round, not totally natural, but that was as it should be, Noki thought. He would not try to make them more lifelike, at least not now.

He heard the far off bells for the evening meal, but kept working until the light faded. He didn't notice the emptiness of his stomach, for his mind was filled with his work. Noki thanked Earth Mother. No matter what had happened to Chinigchinich, Noki felt there would always be an Earth Mother; quiet, subtle, gentle in all that existed.

Noki covered the rocks and trudged up the slope to the mission buildings. Some of the soldiers were singing songs and laughing, but none saw the dark figure near their encampment. With quiet deliberation, Noki entered the church and approached the table where candles flickered. He pulled a small taper from a box and lit it, kneeling and imploring the Sosabitom Gods to heal Father Antonio, his friend. Noki turned to leave and found Father Panella gazing at him, his eyes disapproving.

"You missed the evening prayers."

Noki was too tired to make excuses. "I was thinking about my work, Father, and lost track of time. When I heard the bells, I prayed at the stream." Before the priest could say anything else, Noki slipped away to the men's house where he laid down and quickly fell asleep.

Chapter Twenty

Noki continued working on his project, going out some mornings before Mass, when the sun had barely peeped over the mountains. He also went out after the evening prayers, skipping meals in his quest to get the statue done before Father Antonio returned. Finally, Teresa confronted him, her face stern.

"What are you doing?" she asked. "You work down at the lavandería all day and go back in the evening. You don't eat more than one meal a day. You don't like my food?" she asked, waving her wooden spoon in emphasis.

"Oh, Teresa," Noki said, backing away from the onslaught of her scolding. "I like your food very much. It's delicious."

"Why do you miss meals? You need to fill out that skinny body."

"I . . . it's . . . I am doing something for Father Antonio," Noki stammered.

"Ah, a surprise." Teresa's countenance changed to understanding. "Noki, whatever you are doing, you must still eat. If you don't eat, you will get sick and the surprise will be that Father Antonio will have to bury you when he gets back."

Noki frowned. He needed more time to work alone. He *had* to work during the meals.

"When you miss a meal, come see me after dark and I will have some food saved for you."

"Thank you," he replied, grateful.

She handed him a large corn shuck packet filled with flat bread, overflowing with meat. There was also a roasted ear of corn. "Now go somewhere quiet and rest and eat. Then say your prayers and go to bed."

"Yes, Teresa." She reminded him of Tahmahwit and he felt a quick pang of homesickness.

After that, his work went rapidly. Noki counted the passing days by cutting notches in a stick under his pallet. It had been twenty days so far and there had been no word from Father Antonio. As time passed it became harder to stay patient with the new priest. Father Panella continued urging him to be baptized and did it in a way that irritated Noki.

Noki got up the courage to ask Father José, "When is Father Antonio coming back?"

"I don't know, Noki," the priest replied, his voice uncertain. "It depends on how quickly his injury heals."

"It should not be too much longer, should it?" Noki persisted.

"There is the possibility that Father Antonio's knee will not heal."

Not heal? That was unthinkable. "Why would that be? It healed before. He is a priest. Why wouldn't your gods heal him?"

"That is a very deep question, my son. I don't know why some are cured and some are not. God determines that. But I believe Father Antonio's knee was not totally healed after the first time he injured it. He re-injured it during the fight at your village."

"But still, why wouldn't he be able to come back? He would just have to be more careful."

"It's not that simple, Noki," Father José said as they lugged a large rock over to the dam. After they had positioned it, he pulled off his broad brimmed hat and wiped his brow with his sleeve. "Father Antonio would not be happy sitting and directing, and he wouldn't be happy if he couldn't go to the rancherias to teach."

Noki realized Father José was right. "Do **you** think he will come back?"

"If it is God's will, Noki," Father José repeated. They continued working in silence.

That evening, as Noki was carving on his stone face, he was startled by a slight cough behind him. Jerking around, he saw Tomás, a carrying pouch slung over his shoulder.

Tomás studied Noki's stone for a few minutes. "Father Panella will not like this," he finally said. "He might think it's some kind of idol to our 'heathen gods'. He added sarcastically, "Not that any of them have bothered to learn about our gods." He cocked his head and continued to study the stone face. "You've done a nice job. I can see the beard and you have made the eyes kind; not like there is always pain in them."

Noki paused a moment, taking in Tomás' compliment. "Thank you, but it is not for Father Panella. It's for Father Antonio. And Father Antonio has asked me about our gods."

"How do you know he will return?"

"I feel it. He will return."

"He would have been back by now," Tomás replied, his tone resigned. "Father Panella said today if I am to stay at the mission and I wish to have a place to sleep and food to eat, I must work harder." Tomás changed his voice to mimic the older priest. "Those who enjoy the fruits of the mission should be those who labor for them."

Noki knew his friend was not completely comfortable with life at the mission. Juan told him the only reason Tomás stayed was out of respect for Father Antonio.

Tomás continued, "I am going to the northeast to see if any of my cousins will accept me into their village. The generosity of my kinsfolk is well known."

"I'm sorry to see you leave," Noki replied. Despite the fact that Tomás was considered lazy by the white men, the older boy told wonderful stories of birds, animals and the days of long ago. He could make a grass flute whistle to lure the ground squirrels out of their tunnels and call to the hawks. Best of all, Tomás was always willing to listen to him when he was discouraged.

"You are the only one."

"I know there are others," Noki assured him.

Tomás snorted.

"Father Antonio will be sorry that you left."

"Again, only if he comes back," Tomás insisted.

"He will."

"For your sake, I certainly hope so,"

"Why don't we go to Mission San Juan tomorrow and see if Father Antonio is coming back?"

Tomás gaped at him as though he had sprouted another head.

Noki grinned, pleased with his spur-of-the-moment idea. "If Father Antonio knows how much he is missed, he will come back. If he isn't able to return, you can come with me to my village, because if Father Antonio is not coming back, I will not either."

Tomás' face softened. "I appreciate that, Noki, but do you realize how far it is to Mission San Juan?"

"I have heard this mission was built to make the journey easier for the Spanish traveling the El Camino Real," Noki said. "It should only be a day's walking to the other mission."

"It still gets hot during the day," Tomás protested. "And it's cold in the morning."

"It's not that bad," Noki retorted. "I'm going to talk to Teresa about some extra food for the journey."

"The priests will not like us leaving without asking for permission," Tomás continued.

Why would they care? Noki thought, puzzled. "Tomás, they won't know. We will leave before Mass and be at San Juan by nightfall." The more he thought about it, the more excited he became. Father Antonio would be impressed with their concern and return to the mission with them.

"I don't think it will work."

Noki frowned, irritated with his friend. "You are like the *kanish*, the little ground squirrel that makes large noises but hides at the shadow of a twig." Tomás looked stunned. "If you want to come with me, be here at the first light." When he got to the men's house, there was a plate of food near the fire. Teresa had not forgotten him.

"How is your project coming, Noki?" Juan asked.

Noki hadn't noticed the older man in the shadows when he came in the doorway. "It is going well, Juan." Noki had divulged he was working on something secret, but not what it was.

Noki ate the meal Teresa sent him. As the shadows blended with the night sky, Noki ducked out of the men's house. He hurried over to the cooking area where he found Teresa and handed her the plate.

"Did you enjoy it?" she asked.

"Yes, it was very good, as it usually is." He flashed her a smile.

"It would be much better if you were here to eat it when it's hot," she teased.

"I know." He became more serious. "I have something to ask you."

"What?" She turned to the other women, who were cleaning the pots. "You have done well. You can go now," she told them.

Noki was grateful they were alone. He wanted as few people as possible knowing about his plans. "Could I get some extra food tomorrow morning?"

"Why this sudden larger appetite?"

"I am going to the Mission San Juan after first light."

She sucked in her breath in surprise. "Ah, you are being sent to inquire after Father Antonio."

He didn't correct her supposition. It didn't matter if he had been asked or not; he was going. "It's important to me to find out if he is coming back," he replied.

128

"I think, Noki, if you asked almost anyone here, it would be important to all of us," she said. "I will have a pouch filled with all you will need for a day's journey."

She reached out and enveloped him in her arms. It was almost like when he was Eti's age. He could feel the beating of her heart, as he had his mother's. He was almost a man now and when she loosened her hold on him, he pulled away.

"You will go with my prayers as well as my food," she added.

"Thank you, Teresa. I will be here before the sun breaks above the hills."

The next morning, Noki was up early, approaching Teresa as the other cooks were stirring their pots of corn meal porridge over open fires.

She handed him his breakfast. It was delicious, having been flavored with wild herbs. He finished quickly. "Thank you. That was wonderful."

"It will get you on your way, Noki. Go with God. May your journey find success."

"Thank you. I'm sure it will." Noki slipped out of the enramada. There were no other travelers on the el Camino Real. He listened to the birds calling to each other. Waist high plants waved gently in the morning breezes. The good food and the reason for his quest combined to fill him with contentment.

It was midmorning before he met a lonely traveler. In the distance, he saw a large group of people. They appeared to be Payomkawichum, with a tall, horse drawn wagon behind them. Perhaps, Noki thought, these were people from the Mission San Juan Capistrano and he would get some news of Father Antonio. Maybe Father Antonio would be with them. He broke into a loping run, but stopped when he saw several soldiers on horseback breaking away from the group. They galloped toward him. He looked to one side of the road, but there was little cover. The scrubby plants would not hide him from a man on horseback. The soldiers shouted at him to stand still. There was a deep arroyo to the left of the road. If he could reach that, he would have a chance. Before he got three paces, a horse cut him off.

"Stop there, *peon*," the soldier ordered, the voice deep and harsh.

There was nothing else Noki could do. He heard another horseman behind him, while the third guided his horse to join the two who had penned him in.

The last soldier pulled his horse to a stop and glared at Noki. His light colored beard jutted out in a point from his sharply angular jaw. The man's face could have been carved from stone. "Where are you going?" he snapped.

"I am going to the Mission San Juan Capistrano," Noki answered quickly, not looking away from the hard-eyed soldier, whom he assumed was the leader. Noki struggled to keep from shuddering.

"Who sent you?"

"Uh, I, uh, Father José," Noki replied, thinking the name of the priest might soften the cold eyes. It didn't.

"Where is your paper with the padre's signature on it?"

"Paper?" Noki asked, not having the slightest idea what the soldier was talking about.

"Yes, your paper, idiot! You must have written permission to leave a mission," the soldier said, his voice impatient. The beard bobbed at each word.

Noki had never heard of such a thing. Why hadn't Teresa told him about this? She had said something about one of the priests sending him. The group of Payomkawichum caught up with the soldier and stood behind the soldiers' horses. None of them said anything, but they looked at him with a mixture of curiosity and pity.

"If you don't have papers, you must be a runaway," the soldier declared, motioning one of the other soldiers closer to him. Noki backed up, but couldn't go far without bumping into one of the other soldiers. The horses pranced and bobbed their heads, as though in anticipation of something.

"No, I am going to find Father Antonio at the Mission San Juan Capistrano!" he cried. Then anger flared. "Why do I need a paper saying I can walk on my people's land?"

His voice was drowned out in the pounding of the horse's hooves and Noki began to wonder if the animals were going to trample him. One soldier pulled out a whip and uncoiled it. The end fell to the ground, twitching like it had evil life of its own. The soldier snapped his wrist and the leather suddenly wrapped itself around Noki's neck, pulling him to the ground on his hands and knees.

"It is good to bow to your betters," the soldier snarled.

The whip jerked away, burning as it uncoiled. Next it slashed across his shoulder. Fear paralyzed his feet, but not his tongue. He screamed at the flaming lance of pain biting his shoulder and back.

Suddenly one of the horses squealed in surprise. It danced away from him, bumping into another horse. Noki rolled under the nearest horse and scrambled onto his hands and knees. When the whip didn't strike again, Noki ventured to look up. He saw a rock flying through the air, hitting one of the horses on the rump. It squealed and reared, almost on top of him. The animal towered above him. Noki scrambled farther away and ran off the road toward the arroyo.

"You, boy, come back here!" the soldier leader cried.

Noki ran for the arroyo. His heart thudded and his breath came in sobbing gasps. He didn't care if it angled back in the direction of the Mission San Luis Rey. At least there they didn't beat him or try to trample him with their horses.

Noki ran through thorny brush and felt his shirt rip and shred. He ignored the pain of his abraded skin, and listened for the thunderous approach of the horses. As he ran across the rocks, Noki heard a squeal of pain from the animal behind him. He heard another harsh whinny, but further away. Noki scrambled over boulders and slid on gravel. The sound of the hoof beats receded to a faint rumble and then stopped. Noki looked behind him and saw nothing. He listened and heard only the sounds of insects. After a few minutes, he crawled up the side of the gully and hid behind a gnarled oak. He felt a hand grip his shoulder.

Chapter Twenty-one

At the touch of the hand, Noki almost cried out. He clamped his lips together and pivoted to face his attacker. Before he could do more than take a short breath, Tomás grabbed his wrists. Noki gaped at his friend. Tomás laughed softly but Noki could not join him. He felt humiliated.

Tomás stopped laughing when he saw Noki's face. "You got away. Many of our people have not."

Noki realized what had frightened the horses. "It was you throwing rocks!"

"Yes. I followed you from the mission."

"Why didn't you meet me this morning?" Noki was equally irritated at and grateful to his friend.

"I couldn't decide whether to go to Mission San Juan Capistrano or not," admitted Tomás. "So I followed you. Off the highway, of course. You should have hidden when you first saw the soldiers."

"I didn't realize there were soldiers until it was too late. I also didn't realize that I had to have a paper from a priest." *A piece of paper! Permission to walk his people's lands!* Noki clenched his hands.

"Some priests are so strict they do not let people leave the missions at all," Tomás explained.

Father Antonio had never told him where he could or could not go. The priest had only requested the schedules be followed as closely as possible by those living at the mission. "The soldiers at Father Antonio's mission never do anything."

Tomás snorted. "You are naïve. You have heard about Gabriella, haven't you?"

"Yes." There were whispered rumors, but he had been busy and hadn't inquired about it. All he knew was Gabriella was going to marry a soldier. He could not imagine why a Payomkawichum girl would desire to marry a soldier, but if she wanted to, what was it to him? He said as much to Tomás.

"They were told to marry because the soldier, Adolfo Morales, enticed her to lay under his blanket with him. Now she is pregnant. The priests say if they marry soon, and do penance, they can be absolved." Tomás spat in the dust.

"Penance? Absolved?"

"Penance is doing things to show God you are sorry for the bad choices you have made. Absolved is when the priests and God have forgiven you. It seems Morales is transferring to Los Angeles and is not really interested in marrying Gabriella."

"What will happen to her if there is no wedding?"

"I don't know. It's very hard for a woman who has a baby and no husband to be happy at the mission. Sometimes the baby is taken away to be raised by someone else."

Noki was appalled. "Doesn't she have any family to take her in?" That was the custom in Noki's village when a woman didn't have a husband to care for her and her children.

"I heard one of the women say that Gabriella is ready to go back to her people near the ocean," Tomás said, looking miserable. "I may go with her. I could hunt for her and make sure there is enough meat for her and the child."

"Her family could do that," Noki pointed out. It was then he understood what was behind Tomás' words. "Do you like Gabriella?"

"She is a nice girl, very pretty." Tomás looked away. "Yes, I do," he finally said, his voice almost a whisper. "That was why I didn't meet you this morning. I wanted to make sure she would be all right while I was gone."

"Why don't you marry her? You can adopt her child as your own. If it is a son you would be able to teach him to hunt."

"I don't know if she likes me."

Noki remembered the girl's friendly smile. "Why wouldn't she like you? She seems to like everyone."

Tomás gave a snorting laugh. "Yes, that is true, she does like everybody. But she needs to *really* like only one person. The one who marries her."

"Maybe if you married her, she would like you, at least in that way," Noki suggested.

"Perhaps." He examined Noki, taking in the welt around his neck and shoulders. "That should be washed. We can get the right salves at Mission San Juan tonight."

Noki frowned. Father Antonio had been friendly to him. The soldiers had not. Confusion mired his thoughts. He felt he should have understood everything better. "I am not sure I still want to go."

Tomás shrugged. "We can go to my cousin's village."

Going to Tomás' people was not enticing to him either. He would rather go to his village, but would he be solving his problem? Father Antonio came to his village regularly. Noki thought of the stone face he was working on. He felt good about it, and not just because he wanted to surprise Father Antonio. "I want to talk to Father Antonio. I need time to think. Perhaps we can camp away from the white man's road tonight?"

"I don't want to be away too long, but I think it would be a good thing to spend a night away from the missions."

Noki felt the abrasions pulling, but the sun on his back was warm and the discomfort eased. Some time before the sun set, Tomás found a place to camp. Noki built a fire while Tomás went hunting. Soon he was sitting in front of a small, hot blaze, sharpening the ends of two sticks on which to roast Tomás' kill.

The events of the day still weighed on Noki's mind. *What should I do*, he wondered. Noki threw in several more dead branches. As the sun dipped below the horizon, Tomás reappeared, a rabbit and a ground squirrel dangling from one hand. "These were slow and stupid, and they walked right into my snares," he boasted.

They gutted and skinned the animals, impaling the carcasses on the sticks. The meat roasted while they relaxed. Tomás disappeared again and came back with a large root. Selecting a fist-sized stone, he laid the root on a larger stone and began to mash it into pulp. Noki recognized the medicine plant. It was leather root, a very common remedy. Tomás applied the pulp to the places where the whip had scored. The medicine stung at first, but quickly took the soreness out of Noki's back and neck.

"I remembered it from when my mother was still alive," Tomás explained. "I will mix what's left with some fat from our dinner and apply it in the morning."

Stars appeared, winking and sparkling. Noki said very little during the evening. Tomás was also introspective. By the time the moon rose, Noki felt his eyelids drooping and he curled up near the fire, the chill of the night air forcing him as close as possible. He quickly fell asleep.

He dreamed the same dream he had before. He was on the ocean and the same fish swallowed him. This time, instead of Eti coming to him, Noki saw the stone face he had spent his spare hours carving. For some strange reason he expected it to say something to him.

"Noki," a voice said in his ear. A hand gripped his shoulder and he awoke to darkness.

"What...?"

"You were dreaming," Tomás said. "You called out and woke me."

"Oh. Sorry." Noki shivered, this time from a chill breeze blowing from the ocean.

Tomás threw more branches into the fire. "Nothing to be sorry for. I was half awake from the cold anyway. I think we should sleep closer together," Tomás suggested.

The fire blazed up again and Noki felt comforted by its warmth. A short while later, he and Tomás curled up together. This time Noki had no dreams.

He awoke stiff and cold. Tomás was not beside him. Noki sat up and stretched, greeting the sun rising above the eastern hills.

"About time you woke up," Tomás laughed as he threw dirt on the already dying fire. "There's a stream nearby. Wash up and I will apply more of the leather root before we leave."

The water was cold enough to make his skin crawl, but Noki didn't think about it as he stripped and washed. When he returned to the campsite, Tomás applied the salve. Soon they were on their way toward Mission San Juan.

As they walked on dusty trails, Noki thought of what Tomás had said the previous day about Gabriella. "Are you going back to the mission and talk to Gabriella about becoming your wife?" he asked.

Tomás favored him with thoughtful glance. "Yes, I think I will. I suppose it would not hurt to talk to Father Antonio about her, although if he says no, I will probably go back and ask her anyway."

Noki thought about Maria. She had been in several of his dreams. He remembered her large, deer-like eyes and her soft, melodious voice. Noki shook his head. He had talked with her that one time. It was inconceivable she would remember him. He wondered if she was still at the Mission San Juan.

Noki and Tomás soon came within sight of the El Camino Reál, but didn't walk on it. There were scattered groups of Sosabitom, including some soldiers. They made good time, only stopping to quench their thirst at a stream. Noki caught a small fish and they ate it raw, not wanting to take the time to build a fire. Noki's stomach grumbled, protesting the tiny offering.

The sun had set by the time they walked over the crest of a hill overlooking the Mission San Juan Capistrano. The mission stood in shadow, but lights in some of the windows welcomed the weary travelers.

"Wait here, Noki," Tomás said. "I am going to the men's house and borrow a shirt for you. That way, the priests won't ask any questions."

Noki did as he was told and within a short while, Tomás was back by his side with a clean shirt in his hand.

"I guess you didn't have any trouble getting it."

"I didn't ask. Everyone was eating and this was hanging on a tree limb to dry. We will give it back when it's time for us to leave."

Noki grinned at Tomás' ingenuity. The shirt fit reasonably well and they walked toward an adobe church that showed ghostly white in the deepening twilight. Noki stopped at a large, wooden door. This was so different from the Mission San Luis Rey.

"Come on, Noki. It's just a larger and fancier church. It's been here longer," Tomás said, pulling him through the door.

A young priest stood inside the doorway. "Welcome, my sons. Who sent you here?"

"We are from the Mission San Luis Rey," Tomás responded quickly. "We were sent to inquire after Father Antonio Peyri."

"Father Antonio has finished his evening prayers and is studying and meditating. You two seem worn from your travels and hungry as well. Would you like something to eat before you see Father Antonio?"

"Yes, please, Padre," Tomás said. "It was a long journey and our water and food ran out many hours ago."

The priest beckoned them to follow. Noki leaned over and whispered, "I wanted to see Father Antonio first."

Tomás shushed him with a gesture. Soon they were sitting alone on a bench against the outer wall of a very large men's house, eating their supper. Tomás scooped up his beans with a wooden spoon and bit into a large piece of beef. He ate his meal like a ravenous bear. "The cook here is every bit as good as Teresa back at the Mission San Luis Rey," he said between mouthfuls.

Noki was still irritated that Tomás had spoken for him, but he could see his companion's wisdom. Noki was famished, too.

"We will see Father Antonio in good time, but my stomach was giving me messages I could not ignored."

Noki's irritation vanished with a laugh. Tomás' stomach had been audibly protesting for over an hour. "The priest had a strange look on his face when we told him where we were from. I wonder why?" Noki asked, changing the subject.

"Don't worry about it. For now, enjoy your meal."

Nodding, Noki dug into the food on his plate and soon had finished it. Tomás was dozing against the still-warm adobe wall by the time Noki wiped up the last of his beef gravy.

Chapter Twenty-two

Antonio had just finished his evening prayers when he heard a tapping at his door. He rose from the wooden floor and noted with pleasure that there was no pain in his knee. "Enter."

A young missionary came through the doorway and bowed his head. "There are two neophytes from your mission inquiring after your progress."

Antonio was surprised. Why in the world would Father Panella send anyone to inquire after him when he had so recently dispatched a letter to the priest letting him know his status? "Where are they, Father Miguel?"

"They are in the capilla."

"Thank you. I will see them now," Antonio replied, slipping into his sandals.

Doves cooed in the bell tower, crickets and frogs chirped and sang their varied choruses of the night. A cool breeze from the ocean tugged at his habit. It was much different from the Mission San Luis Rey. As he thought of those differences, he felt a pang of homesickness for the new mission. He had needed this time here in San Juan Capistrano, but he was ready to return to his duties.

Antonio walked into the small room next to the chapel. He paused a moment to let his eyes get used to the glow of the candles flickering on a table along one wall. Two figures on the far side of the room got up from the floor where they had been waiting. Antonio's surprise quickly changed to pleasure at the sight of the two young men. "Noki? Tomás?"

"Father Antonio, you walked in without a limp!"

"Yes, these hot springs here have worked wonders," Antonio replied. He embraced both young men. Noki winced and shifted his body. Antonio noticed a red line along his neck and frowned. It appeared to be a whip burn. "Who did this?" he asked, pointing to the welt.

"A soldier did," Tomás snapped.

"What?" He had given explicit instructions that no one was to use corporal punishment at the mission without consulting with him first. Thus far there had been no need for any. He couldn't believe Noki could do anything to deserve a whipping. "When? Where?" he asked.

"On the Spanish road, Padre. Yesterday," Noki replied.

"Tell me what happened," Antonio said, motioning for the boys to sit down on the bench. Noki began, hesitantly at first, telling how the soldier had jerked him to the ground with his whip and used the lash against his back. Antonio pulled up Noki's shirt and saw the long mark that diagonally striped the boy's back. They had no right to harm this boy! They had been coming to see him. If they had brought a letter from Father Panella, there should have been no problem. "Why were you sent? Father Panella should have received my letter by now."

Tomás snorted. "He did not want us to know that."

Antonio was surprised at Tomás' pronouncement. "Or perhaps he didn't have the chance to tell you. I sent it three days ago." He studied the two neophytes in the dim light. "Did you come on your own?"

"I didn't know a Payomkawichum was not allowed to travel freely on the lands of his people," Noki declared, his anger making his voice crack. "I came here because I was worried you might not come back. Father José could not tell me if you would return." He took a deep breath to calm down. "If you weren't coming back.... I wanted to know."

"I am coming back, Noki. In fact I was going to return within the week." He had a sudden suspicion. "You got along with Father Panella, didn't you?"

"He is not friendly like you. He does not go to the outlying rancherias. Sometimes he is impatient." The boy seemed ready to say more, but didn't.

Tomás coughed. "I am tired, Padre. I am going to find the men's house and go to sleep."

"It is getting late. If you go that way," Antonio said, pointing. "You will find the building where the men sleep. Josef will find you a bed." Although Antonio wanted to talk to Tomás, too, he was glad for the time to speak privately with Noki.

"Noki, I'm sorry the soldiers did this to you. No one deserves to be treated that way."

"And all Father Panella wants to do is baptize me. That is all he talked about," Noki grumbled.

"All I want is to baptize you, Noki," Antonio replied.

Noki stiffened.

"Noki, my beliefs are my most precious possessions. I want to share them with you, my brother." There were several heartbeats of silence. "I want you to have the joy I have," Antonio remembered what had precipitated the

Indian boy's affiliation with the mission. It would be difficult for Noki to feel joy in something that might be perceived as the cause of his recent sorrows.

Noki's voice was almost a whisper. "By joining your church I could lose my family, my friends; my whole way of life.

"Noki, your aunt and uncle have joined the Church. You have not lost them. If you feel you need to talk to your parents about your decisions, by all means go see them. Your father and mother are very good people. I can't imagine them feeling any different in their love for you whatever you decide. Only a small distance separates you from your village friends. And look at the friends you have made at the mission." Antonio stopped to see how the boy was taking this all in. "And your home? Noki, you will have two homes!" The young man relaxed.

"If I decide to join your Church, I want you to baptize me," Noki said.

"You cannot imagine how much that means to me, Noki."

"The baptism will be after we get back to the mission."

"In that case, I need to go back tomorrow," Antonio said with a chuckle.

"You are . . . making fun of me," Noki said, frowning.

"Teasing you? No, I was making a joke, my son. Seriously, that is a very good reason to get back to the mission," Antonio replied. "Perhaps your parents could come." He realized how hard the separation between Noki and his parents had to be for the boy. Antonio was a man when he sailed from Spain, knowing he would never see his parents again. Noki was still a boy. The priest realized he needed to add Noki's parents to his prayers.

"Will they let you come back soon?" Noki queried.

"I don't know why not," the priest answered. "I was told I could return to the mission whenever I felt ready."

Noki frowned as though remembering something unpleasant.

"What is it, Noki?"

"Why does a Payomkawichum have to have permission to walk along paths that were here for him long before your people came?"

Antonio took a few seconds to gather his thoughts for an explanation that would make sense to Noki. How could he explain that most of his countrymen considered the Indian people as nothing more than animals to be caught and broken harshly for service? He couldn't; not right now, anyway. "It was something necessary in the early days. Some of your people were baptized, but afterward they would go back to their old ways and run away. Sometimes they attacked some of my people." Antonio didn't feel he had explained himself very well. Noki's next statement bore that out.

139

"But if they truly believed...."

"Noki, not all are like you," Antonio explained. "Many are baptized before they fully understand the teachings of the Church."

"I have been told that some of my people were forced to receive the baptism—with whips and chains," Noki countered.

This time Antonio sighed. This was something he had debated with some of his fellow priests for several years. "Yes, you have been told rightly, my son. But I swear to you, Noki, by the Holy Mother of God, I will never force you onto a path you do not wish to travel."

Noki was silent for several moments. "But why? Why did your people do this?"

"That seems to be the way with some of my own brethren. They are like soldiers who must conquer a land by whatever means they can."

Noki looked about ready to ask another question, but instead he stared out into the darkness.

"There are some very bloody men out there," Antonio replied before he sat back and took a breath. "Perhaps part of the problem is that we are different, your people and mine, and that which is different is often feared and misjudged."

"Maybe," Noki said. Suddenly, he yawned. The moon had risen; its golden light gleamed through a window and bathed the room.

"It is late. Why don't you go to bed and tomorrow I can show you around this mission," Antonio suggested. "We can talk some more."

Noki yawned again. "Yes, that would be good."

"And Noki, I'm glad you came. It means a great deal to me."

The boy nodded and quietly left.

As Antonio lay down to sleep his heart and soul drew closer to the mission he had been called and set apart to build.

Bells awakened Noki from a sound sleep and a dream where he was stalking game with his father and Uncle Chaht. They were hunting deer, working together to get a prize buck. They were approaching a thicket where it was hiding and that was when the bells tolled. They reached into his dream world and jerked him roughly into the chilly, pre-dawn morning.

Noki sat up and rubbed his eyes. Looking out a window across the room, he saw it was still dark outside. He wondered if the bells had been a dream, too. Everything was silent now, except for the chirping of a few insects. He yawned again and reached for his shirt, hung on a peg over his head.

"That's what you get for staying up so late talking to the priest," Tomás joked from the pallet beside him. He got up, scratching his chest. "They need to do something about these fleas. They kept me awake all night."

Noki felt something crawling on his scalp and he began scratching, too. Apparently they did not clean their bedding here as often as they did in San Luis Rey.

"I think we have plenty of time to bathe before Mass," Tomás said.

"Did they ring the bells? I thought I heard them, but I'm not sure now."

"You heard them."

As Noki stood up, his muscles protested. He had become soft living at the mission. "Maybe we could use the medicine springs."

Tomás clapped him on the back. "You're beginning to think like me, my friend."

Noki grinned. "Thank you. Your cleverness has saved me much trouble in the past few days."

A nearby sleeper muttered a complaint. After they pulled on their pants and shirts, Tomás took Noki by the arm and led him out of the large adobe building. "Let's go before others wake up. Unless the priests have decided to soak this early, we should be the first."

Only the soft lapping of the pungent waters greeted them when they arrived at the springs. Noki slipped off his clothes and entered the warm water. He immersed himself and let the warmth enter his bones. After he soaked for a few minutes, Noki scrubbed his body with his shirt, hoping to clean it in the waters as well. Next he washed his pants, wrung them out and hung them over a large rock. Noki relaxed in the spring while his clothes dried.

He ducked under the water again and washed the trail dust from his hair. When he climbed the stone steps he shivered in the cool morning air. Noki wiped as much water from his body as he could with the heel of his hands and slipped on his damp trousers.

Noki plucked at the damp material, thinking how, less than two months ago, such a thing as these heavy clothes would have been inconceivable to bear. Now nakedness seemed strange. He and Tomás walked toward the church. A young Payomkawichum joined them.

"This is the very church Junipero Serra preached in," the boy said with pride. Noki had heard of this priest; Father Antonio had said he was the founder of the missions of California. He hadn't said anything else about him and Noki didn't ask. He wasn't sure he wanted to know about the white man whose coming had changed his people's lives forever.

They entered the adobe church, dimly lit by candles in sconces. Each sconce hung above a statue. The boy, who introduced himself as Pablo, explained that these were Stations of the Cross. "We do not have these at Mission San Luis Rey," Noki whispered to Pablo. "What is the purpose of these Stations of the Cross?"

"See the statue of Jesus there on the wall?" Pablo asked, pointing to the place inside the door where several people were genuflecting. He continued without any response from Noki. "This represents Jesus being condemned to death by the rulers," Pablo said as he approached the small wooden statue. Like the others, he genuflected and murmured a prayer.

When he got up, Pablo pointed out the other Stations that were at set intervals along the walls, seven on each side. "The next one shows Jesus taking up the cross, and the next when he falls under the weight of the cross as he is going toward the place of crucifixion."

While this was not the part of the story of Jesus that Noki liked to dwell on, he was still curious. "What are the rest?" he whispered.

"Follow me," Pablo whispered back. "I'll tell you."

Pablo took them around the chapel, kneeling and making the sign of the cross and the same prayer at each one. He told them what each represented. The last four stations showed gruesome statues of Jesus suffering and dying, his face contorted in pain.

"If we do these often, it will keep Jesus in our minds and hearts and we will want to do all we can to please Him and His Father."

Noki felt he could remember God Jesus without the horrific reminders of his death, but he kept his thoughts to himself.

"It's almost time to celebrate the Mass," Pablo whispered, guiding them to a place near the front. They sat on the hard-packed earth floor waiting. Several priests came in and sat down close to the main altar. There was an altar at the Mission San Luis Rey, but not as big as this one, nor did it have half so many decorations.

The size of this building! Noki kept looking up at the tremendously high vaulted ceiling, wondering if it was going to fall on him. It appeared too massive for the walls to support it. He couldn't imagine how such a thing could have been built.

Pablo touched him on the arm. "It's all right. The roof is well built and will not fall."

Father Antonio had told him that someday there would be a great church there, too. Noki wondered if it would be this big.

The bells tolled again, their sound echoing inside the church. More people filed in. Father Antonio entered with several other priests. Suddenly Noki's heart caught in his throat.

Despite the headscarf, Noki recognized Maria. She looked every bit as beautiful as she had when he first met her. She did several of the Stations of the Cross before noticing him. When she did, she stopped short. A smile brightened her face. After she sat down with the women she continued to gaze at him. Maria turned to glance at him often during Mass.

When the service was over, Noki went to see her.

"I am surprised to see you here, Noki," Maria said after a short, awkward pause. "But I am happy."

She was happy to see him! Noki tried to say something but his mouth seemed glued shut. He had never acted this way around the girls of his village. What was wrong with him now? Finally, "I am happy, too." He could have kicked himself for saying something so stupid, but he added, "I mean, I am happy to see you, too."

"Surely you didn't come all this way just to see me, did you?"

Noki would have liked to say yes, but he couldn't. "No, I came to see Father Antonio, but I was hoping I would see you here."

"I see you are wearing mission clothes." Maria's colorful skirt gracefully spread around her legs like a large flower.

Noki held out his hand to help her up and she took it. Some of the other girls giggled and Noki could feel his cheeks grow warm. "Uh, I have been at the Mission San Luis Rey for a while," he blurted out.

"They will be serving breakfast soon," Maria said. "Would you like to sit with me?"

"Yes!" They all went together to the enramada where stacks of tortillas and mounds of new oranges lay on several tables. Large pots of corn porridge simmered on the fires. The cooks began spooning out the porridge into small wooden bowls.

There were tables with benches where most of the people sat, but Maria led Noki to a shady place under an arbor of flowers. No one followed them, for which Noki was grateful.

"How is Eti?" Maria asked. "I still have the gift he gave me." She pulled out a small, delicate pink shell strung on a necklace.

Noki's throat constricted. He watched a beetle crawling near his feet before he said anything. "He is dead. He caught the spotted sickness and I took him to the mission to be buried."

"Oh!" She bowed her head and crossed herself. Tears welled in her eyes. "I am so sorry, Noki. I liked Eti. He was very kind to me."

"I miss him, but he has gone on the Starry Path. Father Antonio helped," Noki told her.

"Is that why you like Father Antonio?"

"That is one reason." Right now, Father Antonio was the farthest thing from his mind. Noki liked Maria as he had never liked a girl before. He enjoyed her smile, her expressive eyes, her laugh, and the soft deepness of her voice. His eyes traveled upward to the white blouse and he watched a moment as her chest rose and fell. As she breathed, the polished wooden beads of her necklace shifted in the hollow between her breasts. Noki felt stirrings he had never experienced before. It was strange and exciting at the same time.

Noki looked up at Maria's face and saw her studying him, her food untouched. He felt his cheeks grow warm again. He tried to compose himself. "Where is your village?" he asked.

"Here at the mission," she answered hastily. He wondered if she was feeling the same way he was.

"Oh, I figured that," Noki replied, realizing his mistake. "I mean what place are your people from. Around here, I mean. Uh, which village?"

"My mother and brother and I came from a village north of here, near the sea."

Noki felt a bit more comfortable now. "Was it like the place near where we met?" he asked.

"Something like that, although we weren't quite that close to the ocean," she replied. "Sometimes the wind in the grass was louder than the surf, but we always felt the cool softness of the ocean mists and smelled the tangy salt scent of the water." She looked wistful. "My father died of the spotted sickness that killed many members of our people," she said in the Payomkawichum language.

"Oh," Noki replied, feeling awkward again. "I'm sorry for the loss of your father." He looked at his now cold bowl of porridge. "We were lucky. Only a few in our village caught it. Kawawish said it was the curse of the white man."

"Perhaps Kawawish is right," she said. "This sickness was unheard of before they came." She leaned forward. "They don't like to think that, though. Maybe because they might feel badly."

"Are you happy here, Maria?" Noki blurted out after another short silence.

"Oh, yes," she said brightening, as though ready to leave the unpleasant subjects behind. "I learn things I would never have learned otherwise. So that I don't forget the old ways, Mother tells me the stories of our ancestors." She brushed her hand around her skirt and the embroidered pictures at the bottom. "Do you like this?"

"It's beautiful," Noki replied, leaning down to look closer. His fingers touched the designs and he felt the warmth of her leg underneath. Noki jerked his hand away when he felt the stirrings inside his body again. Maria didn't seem to notice his discomfort.

"I made up the designs from the old stories. Some of them were in my dreams and when I woke up, I sewed them on the material," she said, proud of her handiwork. "Father Gregorio said I have great gift. I embroidered the hem of his new alb."

Noki was impressed. He had admired the drawings on her skirt, the bright and happy colors and the way they flowed along the material. They were like birds in flight. He had seen such detail and design in baskets that his mother and some of the other women wove, but never with such bright colors.

"Yes, Mamá has told me that I have a great talent," she said. Her cheeks brightened with embarrassment. "I shouldn't be boasting. It's unseemly."

Noki leaned over and touched her hand. "Why? People should be proud of their talents. You should be happy at what you do."

"Thank you. I have always made designs. Even as a little girl."

He thought of his own efforts back at the lavandería. They seemed clumsy in comparison. He reached into his pouch and pulled out his last good arrowhead, handing it to her. "I made this," he said. "My father is a weapon maker."

Maria turned it over and over, gazing at it. "This is very nice, but aren't you afraid that it will lose power by letting me handle it?" she asked.

"No, I have not been able to see into the arrowhead stones for several weeks now. My father approved this before that time. At the mission there doesn't seem to be a need for such a thing."

"You intend to stay at the Mission San Luis Rey?" Maria asked.

Chapter Twenty-three

"I don't know," Noki said, thinking of his family and remembering his encounter with the soldiers. When he saw her disappointed look he added, "I haven't decided yet. Father Antonio took me with him when he visited some of the outlying villages."

"He goes out and visits villages? You mean the villages close by, don't you?"

"No, outlying villages, like the one I came from. It takes four or five hours to walk from my village to the mission. At least it takes Father Antonio five hours. He teaches and baptizes. I have helped him tell stories. It's hard sometimes, because the shamans hate him and some of the people fear him, but still he teaches and baptizes."

"They don't come to the mission after they are baptized?"

"Some do, but most do not. Father Antonio holds a mass when he can. Or he did before he came here."

Maria's look was one of surprise.

"Don't they do that here?" he queried.

"No, not really. People are encouraged to live here."

"I think my uncle liked it that he could be baptized and still live in the village. So did Captain Oomaqat. They can live pretty much like they always have. But it's hard for the priests to go out at times."

"I can imagine." She held his arrowhead out to him.

"No, you keep it. It's a gift. I want you to have it."

Maria rubbed her thumb along the edges. "I will put this on the necklace with Eti's shell, if that's all right."

Noki was proud she would do that. "That would be fine. Would you like me to make a hole in it for you?"

"Yes, please." She placed the arrowhead in the palm of his hand.

Maria's fingers lingered on his hand; warm but strong. As she drew away, her fingertips caressed his. Noki felt a tingle of excitement run through his body.

"It is still good to have something to hunt with," she pointed out. "So your talent in making arrowheads would not be wasted. Some of the people go into the hills and hunt for animals like quail and rabbits when we are tired of mission food."

Noki nodded, but he was still staring at the arrow point in his hand. She liked his gift and wanted to keep it around her neck with Eti's gift. He wondered if she or her mother would be offended if he gave her something else. Before he could say anything, the bells tolled.

"It's time to go to work."

Noki glanced at his uneaten food. Maria's was untouched, too. He bolted down a tortilla as she did the same. "We'll be very hungry by lunch," he observed.

Her laughter was like the soft rippling of spring water over the rocks. "When we get together for lunch, we'll have to make sure we eat as well as talk."

Noki felt another thrill in his chest. Maria left to join the women and girls who spun carded wool into yarn, made fabric, and sewed designs on the finished cloth. Not knowing what else to do, Noki went in search of Father Antonio. The priest took him on a tour of the Mission San Juan. The completed adobe chapel was impressive enough, but when the priest showed him the construction of a larger church, his mind boggled. The earth had been dug out for the foundation of the walls and huge quantities of stone were piled nearby. Stoneworkers chipped stones to the right size. Others placed them one on top of another. Workers put mortar around the stones, so they would stay in place. Some of the stones fit so well together, the mortar was not necessary. "Are you going to build a church like this one?" Noki finally asked.

"No, I don't think so, my son. I believe it will be quicker to construct a building out of adobe than out of stone. I envision a grand adobe church." Father Antonio answered. "Despite what I have been told, I think it will endure for many generations."

Noki thought the priest was right. The walls of the church at his mission were almost half done. His mission? Had he become so used to living at the white men's rancheria that he was now calling it "his" mission? Despite things that sometimes confused him, despite what had happened on the white man's road, he was comfortable at the place Father Antonio had built.

Still, Noki yearned to see his parents. Soon it would be time for the fall acorn harvest. He wanted to sit with Father at the campfire, talking about making arrowheads. He could almost hear Atu's babbling in the background.

Noki was ready to go through the manhood rituals. After he was a man, he could think of making Maria his wife. Noki almost stopped in his tracks at that thought. Marriage? It was right and proper after the manhood ceremonies to think of finding a wife. Not right away, but soon. Would Maria consider such a thing? Might she possibly want to go with him and live in his village? His mind churned and he didn't pay attention to where he was or what Father Antonio was saying.

"Noki?"

Noki jerked back to the present. "I'm sorry, Padre. What did you say?"

"You looked to be somewhere far away, my son," the priest said with a soft chuckle. "I was asking what you thought of the bells. I think we should have four. What do you think?"

Noki grimaced. "I think the one at your mission is enough, Father. Such things are unknown to our people and...." Noki paused, unable to think of a polite way to let the priest know how much he disliked the bells. "Even one is hard to get used to."

"Hmm, I think you're right. The one we have is quite loud." They walked in silence for a few minutes, listening to the birds twittering. "I picture a large bell tower for our bell."

Noki, who had seen some of Father Antonio's drawings, thought he knew what the priest was talking about. "You mean that tall thing in front of the large building you drew?"

"Yes."

"People would be able to see that from a great distance."

"Yes, travelers as well as local people."

Father Antonio took him inside the large chapel where Mass had been held. Now Noki had more time to study the details of each decoration. The statue of Jesus looked so real. Noki decided his stone face could not come close in comparison. He wondered why he presumed to be able to do such a thing. Father Antonio would never care for it.

"It is beautiful, isn't it?" the priest said.

"The person carved in great detail," Noki agreed. "It makes me sad."

"It's supposed to make us sad. We are meant to remember the suffering our Savior went through for us," Father Antonio replied.

"But wasn't he sometimes holding children on his lap and teaching them?"

There was a pause. "Yes, Jesus did enjoy being with children, Noki. He loved to teach and heal and help."

As he looked at the statue, Noki wanted to climb up, take Jesus down from the horrible wooden cross and hold him in his arms. He wondered if such a thought would offend the Great God of the white men? Somehow, he didn't think so.

"Shall we see a bit more? There is time before the mid-day meal," Father Antonio said.

"Yes, I would like that very much, Padre."

The priest took him to where many candles were lit. Noki picked up a small candle and lit it from those that were burning already.

"For Eti?" Father Antonio asked, his voice solemn.

"Yes." Noki still had yet to burn sweet sage for his brother. He could do it at the acorn harvest.

"He would appreciate it."

They went into another room that was more alcove than actual room. There, Noki saw a metal basin set on top of a stone base. The metal was polished to a high sheen and he was mesmerized by it. It was the brightness and color of the sun near the end of the day. On one side of the metal bowl, there was a small receptacle, also made out of metal. It was a different color, a shiny white, almost like the color of the sea before a storm. It looked like the baptismal font at their mission, but with more shiny metal.

"Are they always the same?" Noki asked. He envisioned something like this, but made of stone set with some of the beautiful colored gems he had seen in the altar where the priest said Mass. He saw it in his mind clear and distinct.

"No, some are more simple than this, some more ornate. Come, let me show you the rest of the church." Noki followed as they walked to another part of the room. A massive wooden stand held an equally massive book. Noki had seen a variety of books at the Mission San Luis Rey, but none were so big. He had seen Father Antonio looking at a tiny one he carried in his small pouch. Now he studied the large book. It was open; its large pages showing designs on one side and a picture on the other. He wondered about the designs. His people's designs showed animals, people and events, the stars, the moon and the sun, but these had no meaning to him. The picture, though, was different. It, like the statue in the chapel, was detailed and very colorful.

He reached out, almost touching it. There was a group of men in the picture and Noki recognized the story. It was what Father Antonio had called the Last Supper. Jesus' followers were in attitudes of rapt attention or devotion, except for the betrayer, the one who had caused the death of the Son God. Noki studied the picture. Pulling his eyes away, he studied the designs, trying to make sense out of them. Some were larger than the others, some flowed into the next ones and there were dots here and there. "Father Antonio, what do these designs mean?" he finally asked.

"They are letters. Groups of letters make words," the priest explained.

Letters, words? Noki thought, confused.

Father Antonio recognized his confusion. He pointed and began reading. It was the story that was in the picture but with more detail.

"This is where you get the stories?" Noki asked, entranced.

"Yes, my son, it is."

"And you know how to make sense of these de . . . letters and words?"

"Indeed I do. I studied and learned to read them."

Noki looked up from the book and saw Father Antonio watching him. "Is it hard to learn to . . . read these words?"

"At first, Noki, but it becomes easier. Would you like to learn?"

Noki remembered similar designs under some of Father Antonio's drawings, but he had never thought about them before. But now? Now he was eager to know what those 'words' meant, to learn about the drawings, the pictures and the stories for himself. "Is that what you are doing when I see you with paper and paint?"

Father Antonio chuckled. "Ink, Noki, not paint. And it is. I am writing words, telling others what is going on at the mission. I send words all the way to my home in Spain, so my family knows what I am doing."

"And the words tell the same things the pictures do?"

"Words can tell much more than pictures and they are easier to put on the paper. At least for me."

Now Noki laughed. "But Father Antonio, your drawings of buildings are so . . . so real."

"Yes, the buildings are, but I cannot make drawings like this one here," he said, pointing to the picture in the book. "I can use words on paper to tell about it."

"Like you use words in the villages to tell stories about the God Jesus," Noki said, excited.

"It is the same, but words on paper can be read over and over again by many people, even after the person who wrote them is dead."

Noki could not take his eyes off the book. "Yes, Father, please. I would very much like to learn to read letters and words."

"When we get back to the mission, I will teach you."

Noki felt shivers of anticipation run up his back. "Thank you," he said.

Maria invited Noki to sit with her during lunch. Tomás grinned and moved off to sit with a small group of young men. It was an unusually hot day, but a slight breeze from the ocean made it tolerable. Noki took a bite of his food and wondered what to talk about. Like before, he could not help noticing Maria's womanly attributes, though he tried to be as discreet as possible.

"What have you been doing at the mission? Your mission?" Maria asked, "Besides helping Father Antonio teach in the villages."

"Working wherever I'm needed. We are building a lavandería."

"Already?"

"Yes," Noki replied, warming to the subject. "There is a wood roof on the church and the foundation has been laid for a larger church. We are building a larger men's house, and the first crop of corn has been harvested. The wheat will soon be ready for harvest."

Maria was clearly impressed. "I knew that Father Antonio wanted to build his mission quickly, but I didn't know he was that determined."

Noki wished Maria could live at the mission with him. He felt comfortable around her, more comfortable than he did with anyone his age. "He has shown me his drawings. He wants to build a chapel like the one you have here, but bigger, with a large bell tower and big adobe walls. He wants buildings for a tannery and granaries. He says there should be smaller churches in places like my village."

"Do you think he can do all this?"

"Yes. He has been learning our language for when we visit the villages in the hills." His voice trailed off and there was a prolonged and awkward silence. He wondered what Father would think of what he was doing now. He wondered what he would think of Maria.

"You came to find Father Antonio," Maria began.

"Yes." He didn't know what else to say.

"So will you be going back to the Mission San Luis Rey or to your village?"

Noki hesitated a moment. Despite his previous excitement, he felt a twinge of uncertainty. He remembered a time not too long ago when all he lived for was to follow his father's line of work. Now? He wasn't sure how he felt. He reached into his pouch and pulled out the arrowhead. Just before lunch, he had drilled a small, round hole at the top. He handed it to Maria.

"You have a wonderful talent." She untied the knot on her necklace and strung the arrowhead on it.

"I chipped it to the right size," he replied, trying to sound nonchalant about it, but pleased at her praise.

"Noki, to make something this balanced and perfect takes real talent. Have you ever made anything besides weapons? Maybe carved something, like an animal?"

Noki hesitated, wondering if he should tell her about his stone carving of the face of Jesus at the lavandería. "I have tried carving animals out of deer antler," he admitted.

"I imagine they were good, too. Use this talent, Noki. It is a gift from God."

Noki was startled. His father had told him his abilities came from the gods. "Do you really think so?"

"Yes!"

Again Noki felt warm inside. "I wish you were living at the Mission San Luis Rey," he blurted.

"Why?"

Noki paused. "Because you are nice," he finally stammered. "And you're, uh, fun to be around."

"Thank you. I enjoy being around you, too."

"Have you...." he began and blushed, having been about to ask her if she had thought about marriage. "You have a wonderful talent, too," he said, returning to a safe topic.

Maria glanced down at the small designs on her skirt. "I learned from my mother."

"Would you be able to come to Mission San Luis Rey to my baptism?" he asked, realizing he did indeed plan on being baptized someday.

Maria looked surprised. "You aren't baptized?"

Noki shook his head. "No, I wasn't sure. I have to . . . uh...." He didn't want to bring up the problem with his father, but his eyes must have mirrored his distress.

"What's wrong, Noki?" Her voice was soft and the hand lying on his arm was comforting.

"I took Eti's body to the mission without asking my father," he responded, almost in a whisper.

Maria drew in her breath. "Why?"

Noki explained the circumstances as briefly as he could.

"And your parents?" she asked.

"They came to the burial, but left right after. They are living with relatives in the mountains."

It was quiet for several minutes. "I think you need to talk to your father before you are baptized. He probably misses you as much as you miss him." Maria's eyes brimmed with tears. "I don't have a father. I have often wondered what it would be like to speak to him. I remember him as a very large man, who could carry my brother and me on his shoulders with great ease. He laughed a lot and liked to tell stories of the old days and the gods." Her hand encircled his wrist. "Talk to your father. Let him know your heart. If he is anything like my father, he will listen and your hearts will come closer together."

Even though Uncle Chaht had made the same assurances, it was good to hear it from Maria, too. He realized he had said only a few words and she seemed to understand so much. "That is how I feel. Father told my uncle he would talk with me during the acorn gathering time."

"That is wonderful, Noki! Your father still cares for you. After you have visited with your parents and you're ready for your baptism, send word and I'll come. But don't wait too long," Maria added.

Noki's heart beat faster. "I won't," he replied. Her dark eyes seemed like calm pools.

"I will always come if you need me, Noki," she said. "You are special."

"Sp . . .special?"

"There is something of the eagle and the bear in your heart and the gentle deer in your soul. I like you for all of those things," she said. "I felt that the first time I met you when you came with Eti."

"You did?" he asked, self-conscious.

"I did."

"When we are old enough, will you marry me?"

Maria didn't laugh. She didn't even smile. Her countenance was serious. "I will, if you still feel the same way in a few years."

Noki couldn't believe he had proposed and he couldn't believe she had said yes.

"And when you are baptized...."

"Yes?" he prompted when she paused.

"When you are baptized, do not change your name to a Spanish one like so many do."

"Why not?" Noki had always thought his name a bit less than stellar, much preferring a dignified one; something from a fierce animal or bird like his father's name.

"It means "my house" does it not?"

153

"Yes," he said hesitantly.

She touched his chest where his heart lay. "Remember your house holds what makes you who you are. I like who you are."

Noki could say nothing for a very long time. Finally, the bells rang for the next part of the day.

The return to the Mission San Luis Rey the following day was pleasant and without incident. As they walked along the highway, Father Antonio, Tomás and Noki talked of many things. The soldier accompanying them walked his horse behind them. At times he almost appeared to be dozing, but that suited Noki just fine.

He remembered what the soldier leader on the El Camino Real had called him--"an ignorant savage." Noki had been too busy trying to save himself to consider the words. But later, after they had reached the Mission San Juan Capistrano, he pondered the words. He didn't understand them, but knew they weren't flattering. Noki asked Father Antonio what the soldier meant.

"According to my race, there are two kinds of people here, Noki," Father Antonio said. "There are the semi-barbarians—your people. The Payomkawichum who are gentle and easy to be taught and who will work hard. There are also the *gente de razón*, the so-called people of reason, my people. These include the ranchers and soldiers, many of whom are idle, and glut off the labor of others. They live for pleasure, wine and gambling." Father Antonio had to explain in more detail what he meant, but Noki easily understood the priest's disgust. "I used to think the same way until I came to your land. Now I'm seeing just how special your people are." He paused. "It's hard to change a lifetime of beliefs in such a short time."

"It's very hard, Father." Noki agreed. They walked for some time in silence, and Noki concentrated on the sound of their footsteps and the thudding of the horse's hooves.

Chapter Twenty-four

"I want to marry Gabriella," Tomás declared, surprising Antonio with his bluntness.

He stopped short and Noki almost bumped into him. "I think it's time for a rest," Antonio said. The soldier was watching them. "Corporal, there is a stream less than a quarter of a league to the south. Go ahead and let your horse rest and get a drink. We will catch up with you in a little while."

"But Father...."

"We'll be fine and if there's any trouble you will be able to hear our calls for help."

The soldier didn't argue and soon was out of earshot.

"Do you wish to speak privately about this, Tomás?" Antonio asked.

"No, Padre. Noki knows all about how I feel, and . . . and he's almost as old as I am."

"All right, let's sit under that tree," Antonio directed. Soon they were all sitting in the shade. Antonio passed around the water skin. "Tomás, why do you wish to marry Gabriella? Do you love her?"

"I like her a lot, Father."

"I guess I don't have to tell you she's pregnant." Antonio knew how gossip spread in a mission.

"No, Father. I already know. That is one reason I want to marry her. I . . . I, uh, want her to have a good life. I want to take care of her . . . and her baby."

"You are old enough to know the rules in these matters. The person who has made the girl pregnant is the one who should marry her." Antonio paused to word the next question carefully. "Tomás, there is a question I need to ask you."

"Father, I think I know what it is. No, I haven't slept with Gabriella. I swear by the Bible you teach from."

"I didn't think you had." Antonio felt new respect for the young man next to him. "Private Morales is the one who should marry her."

"He does not want her! He has not seen her since he received orders to go to San Diego."

Antonio was surprised. "He received orders?"

"Yes, Padre," Tomás said. "Father Panella told Private Adolfo to marry her, but he got his orders to leave and he has not married her. Someone said he heard Morales say if he was forced to marry her, he would let her be the barracks girl in San Diego."

A barracks girl? After doing the laundry and other chores for the soldiers, Gabriella would likely be the *puta*, or prostitute for any soldier there. How could a young girl be treated like that? The sacrament of marriage entailed fidelity of the couple and should not be sullied in such a way.

"Gabriella doesn't deserve that, Father," Tomás broke into his thoughts. "Her baby doesn't deserve that!"

So Tomás had heard about barracks girls. "You really care for her, my son?" Antonio asked again.

Tomás took a deep breath. "Yes, Father, I do." He paused. "I want her to have happiness."

Antonio could see the sincerity in the young man's eyes. "Having a wife and baby to care for is not easy."

"I know, Father Antonio. I will work hard and I will treat the baby as though it were my own. If Gabriella will have me as her husband, I will adopt the baby." There was a pause. "I know I haven't worked like you have wanted me to, but if you will let me marry Gabriella I will do anything I can to take care of her. Anything rather than let her become a . . . a dog to the soldiers!"

Antonio sat back and thought a minute. He didn't want to say anything hasty. Somehow he felt this young man would be a very good father to the baby and a loving husband to Gabriella. God knew she deserved some happiness in all of this. "Tomás, I agree with you, but there is the problem of everyone knowing the details of Gabriella and Pvt. Morales. That might make it difficult for her to continue to live at the mission."

"I can take her to my cousins' village," Tomás suggested.

"Hmm," was all Antonio said. He really didn't want to lose all contact with Gabriella or Tomás.

"I am sure my Uncle Chaht and Aunt Sachac would adopt Tomás and Gabriella into their family," Noki suggested, as though reading Antonio's mind. "They don't have any children. Tomás and Gabriella and the baby could live in my village and we could visit each other any time. Once the captain has agreed, no one can disagree."

Tomás smiled for the first time since his big surprise announcement. "Please, Father. I would like that very much."

"I think it is a wonderful idea, but we can't speak for your aunt and uncle, Noki. And we can't speak for Gabriella. I also need to pray on the

156

matter and see what God's will is. Soon you will have an answer, Tomás, I promise."

The rest of the journey went well and they arrived at the mission in time for the evening prayers. Antonio stopped in his tracks when he saw the progress that had been made. The walls of the new chapel were at least six feet tall, beyond the mere footings that had been there when he left. The women's building had been measured out according to his specifications and was ready for the adobes to be laid.

Father José Panella greeted him warmly and frowned at the two young men at his side.

Antonio reassured his fellow cleric. "They have been duly chastised, and have done their penance, Father." He turned to the two young men. "Tomás, you go and talk with Gabriella. Noki, tomorrow, after Mass, we will all talk together and then you can make a trip to your village to talk to your uncle and aunt." The two young men grinned and ran off.

The children realized he was back and soon the priest was surrounded. He laughed and hugged as many as he could. "Children, accompany me to the church," he called out.

As more people realized he was back, the procession became larger until it seemed the entire mission was gathered around him.

Antonio sat in his small room with Fathers Panella and José. He was tired, but he wanted to get a partial report before he went to bed. "You have done magnificently. This is a blessed work and we all have been given strength by God."

The men gave reports on the damming of the spring, building the stairs to the lavandería, the construction of the larger church, baptisms of new neophytes and impending marriages.

Antonio noticed the absence of information of visits to the outlying rancherias, but he said nothing. Indeed, he really couldn't. So much had been done at the mission while he was away. After each priest had given his report, Antonio asked about Gabriella. Father Panella gave him the details. It was as Tomás had related. "What has been done about the situation thus far?"

"I have talked with the soldier," Father Panella said. "And told him of the dire consequences of unrepentant sin. Private Morales said he would marry Gabriella in San Diego."

Antonio frowned. The answer wasn't to his liking. He suspected Morales would never marry the poor girl. Her life in San Diego would be hell.

After his missionary brethren left for their own rooms, Antonio pondered. Restless, he got up and walked to the soldiers' tents. Most of the men were sitting around a fire, smoking and, he suspected, drinking too much wine. One of the men on the outskirts of the firelight saw him approaching.

"Father!" the soldier said in a loud voice. The cursing and jokes ceased. "What a pleasant surprise. What can we do for you?"

"I wish to speak to Private Morales," Antonio said. "Tell him to come to the church." Without waiting for an answer, he turned and walked back.

Antonio sat near the altar waiting for the young man. When Morales arrived, the candles illuminated a young face. The soldier was probably not more than eighteen, possibly twenty, Antonio thought. *Still, he is old enough to know better!* Morales' sandy brown hair was disheveled. His gray eyes flicked back and forth between the altar and the priest's face. Leather helmet in his hand, Morales bowed his head and stood quietly. The priest said nothing for a while.

"You wished to speak to me, Father?" Morales asked after several moments of silence.

"Yes, I did," Antonio replied. "I want to know what you intend to do about the sin you have committed." In the dim light of the flickering candles, it was hard to see what was on the soldier's mind.

"Sin, Father?" Morales said, his eyes still flicking. "Someone lied when they said I had slept with the Indian. Father Panella kept asking and...."

"I said nothing about an Indian," Antonio said, continuing to study the young soldier's face. "And I have no intention of arguing with you or listen to you lie to me. You both sinned. Father Panella tried to help you, but it would seem you are not ready."

Morales still would not look Antonio in the eye. "I will help the Indian girl. I will marry her."

"And how did you intend to take care of her? Do you have a family in Alta California you could send Gabriella to?"

"No," Morales said.

"The girls and women here are not for your pleasure!" Antonio snapped, feeling any further questions useless. "I am trying to teach these people about Christ and how to live Christian lives. You, Private, are supposed to be a member of the Holy Mother Church. What example are you setting by this kind of behavior?" Antonio felt his anger build. It would do no good to lose his temper in front of Morales. "I want you on your way to San Diego at first light."

Morales stared at him, his jaw hanging in shock.

"Go! Send me your commanding officer."

Morales stood there for a moment, but finally left at the wave of Antonio's hand. Soon Lieutenant Cabal came in, pausing to genuflect halfway to the altar.

"Lieutenant, I would like you to accompany Father Panella to the Mission San Diego tomorrow morning. He has indicated his desire to return to his offices as quickly as possible. I would like Private Morales to accompany you."

"What about the Indian girl, Padre?" Cabal asked.

"That is my concern," Antonio retorted. "And Father Panella will take care of Private Morales. I would also like you to impress upon your soldiers not to take pleasure with any women other than their wives." He paused, gazing hard at the lieutenant. "Have I made myself clear?"

"Yes, Padre," Cabal said, nodding his head in deference.

"Thank you," Antonio replied. After the soldier left, the priest knelt in front of the crucifix on the wall. He took a few moments to calm himself.

Later, as he lay down on his narrow bed, Antonio recalled that Noki had been absent during the evening vespers. Father Panella mentioned the young man had been absent from prayers and dinner a great deal of the time. He also remembered Father José mentioning how hard Noki had been working. *What is he up to?* Antonio's curiosity was aroused.

Though he had been away for just five days, Noki was anxious about his project. He dashed down to the place where he had hidden his stones. Pulling off the brush, Noki saw nothing was changed. At the top of one of the stones, the large eyes were round and gentle. At the bottom the curved upper lip was adorned with a moustache. The top stone was almost finished. The features of the bottom stone were chipped out, but he needed to add the details to the beard.

Beards had been something hard for him to picture until he had seen a soldier with a beard. The men in his tribe had very sparse chin hair, which was plucked out with mussel shell tweezers. In every drawing, every statue he had seen, either here or at San Juan Capistrano, the Son God, Jesus had a beard. Noki thought about what he had seen at the other mission and about his own statue. Yes, his was not as detailed as those others, but still, he could see the white god's face in it and picture it complete and put together.

Noki pulled out his tools from their hiding place and began chipping. A little on the edges of the mouth and shallow lines to show details in Jesus' beard. There was a little chiseling needed to make the two parts of the face match.

Finally, Noki stood back and studied his efforts. They would fit together very well, he thought. To test his theory, Noki decided to stack the stones. He took a deep breath and wrapped his arms around the middle stone. He grunted with the effort of lifting it. After he laid the stone on top, he stepped back and studied it. The lips fit perfectly. The sun shone over his shoulder in a deep reddish-gold glow, illuminating the features of his creation. Noki gasped at the effect. The sunlight softened the contours of the eyes making them seem alive. He expected the mouth to start speaking. As the twilight set in, Noki realized how late it was. He barely got back in time for dinner.

"I hoped you would be back soon!" Teresa cried out when she saw him.

"I'm glad to be back," Noki replied. He took his food and sat with his friends, telling them some of his adventures at the other mission. By the time he had finished his dinner, his feet were stumbling over dirt clods. It was not long before he was in the men's house fast asleep.

Noki felt the light touch of a hand on his shoulder. His eyes popped open to complete darkness. He flinched from the touch, but stayed silent when he heard a very soft 'shh.'

"Tomás?" he whispered.

"Yes. Come with me," came the reply in his ear.

With only the slightest of sounds, Noki rose to his feet and followed his friend, grabbing the shirt by his pallet. Noki looked upward at the stars and figured it wasn't more than a few hours after sunset. "Anything wrong?"

"Gabriella said she would marry me!" Tomás crowed.

"That's wonderful!" Noki replied. "I'm sure Uncle Chaht will take you two in, too."

Tomás sobered. "Gabriella is worried someone will keep Father Antonio from marrying us. She wants to leave now and go to a faraway village."

"Father Antonio is in charge here. Who would tell him you two couldn't marry?"

Tomás sighed. "I don't know. Sometimes the priests are more bound by their rules than by sense. Father Antonio has leaders above him, too."

"Don't you think Father Antonio knows about the rules? He wouldn't have promised to help you if he couldn't."

"I feel that way, too, Noki. Maybe if you tell Gabriella she'll believe you. She's waiting for me at the enramada."

Noki followed Tomás to where the girl was pacing along the inner wall. She jumped when he called out to her. Noki repeated what he had said to Tomás.

"I am carrying a Sosabitom's baby," Gabriella cried. "And I have heard stories."

"What stories?" Noki asked.

"Stories about the priests sending soldiers to capture those who leave the missions and run away," she whispered.

"Do you really think Father Antonio would do that?" Noki asked, incredulous. "Besides, he liked the idea of you and Tomás living in my uncle's village."

"No, I don't think *he* would, but maybe Morales' leaders would come after me to get the baby. Or some other priest."

Noki snorted. "What would soldiers want with a baby?"

"When he is old enough, he will be someone else to polish the soldiers' boots or clean up after them," Gabriella replied with a sniffle.

Noki was taken aback by the emotional answer, even though he didn't believe it was realistic. "Father Antonio wouldn't have made a promise if he couldn't keep it. He could marry you two and you'd be gone before anyone else knew. Father Panella is leaving tomorrow morning with Private Morales."

"Are you sure?" Gabriella asked, wiping her eyes with the sleeve of her blouse.

"I'm sure," Noki and Tomás said at the same time.

"I'm afraid of him," Gabriella whispered.

"Private Morales?" Tomás asked.

She nodded.

"I won't let him come near you," Tomás said. "I will stand guard outside the women's house."

"I will help," Noki added.

Chapter Twenty-five

Antonio awoke before dawn, prayed, and washed in the tiny basin. Eager to see everything that had been accomplished during his absence, he slipped out into the cool half-light. He walked down the trail to the river and stood very still, listening to the water play over the rocks. It was a pleasing, tranquil sound. Landscape features became more distinct as the sun approached the horizon.

Antonio saw where stones had been gathered for the dam as well as the steps lining the steep walkway to the lavandería. In a nearby stand of trees he saw several large stones stacked on one another. The top stone formed the upper half of a face. The eyes were almond shaped, perfectly matched in size with round, recessed brows arching high over the eyes. The upper part of a mouth matched perfectly with the lower part of the mouth on the second stone. The bottom stone was uncarved and served as the base. Although primitive, Antonio was impressed by its beauty.

Walking up and lightly touching the face, Antonio realized the figure represented Jesus Christ. It was so different from the suffering Christ on the cross that hung in the church. Yet it was just as powerful. As he examined the carved stone, Antonio pondered the insight of its creator. He heard a noise behind him, turned and saw Noki.

Antonio realized who had done the work on the stones. He figured the boy had worked alone. Noki stared at him, waiting. Antonio returned his gaze to the statue and said, "You have done a magnificent job of depicting the personality of the Holy Son of God." He turned to Noki again and saw a faint smile on the boy's lips. "And with such hard stone." Antonio wasn't sure what kind of stone it was, but it wasn't the soft sandstone he had seen in Mexico. That the boy would use such materials bespoke of Noki's determination as well as his talent.

"I didn't know if you would like it. I have been working on it since you left. It was to be a surprise."

"It **is** a surprise," Antonio said. "You have done a wonderful job in such a short time. You are incredibly talented."

"I did? I am?"

Antonio could see the tension draining from the boy's body. "May I ask what you were thinking about while you were working on your sculpture?"

"I thought of the story you tell of Jesus teaching the children. I imagined Him telling stories about the birds of the sky and the foxes of the fields, about heaven...." Noki stopped and choked back a sobbing breath. He swiped his hand over his eyes.

"What is it, my son?" Antonio asked, concerned.

The tears began trickling down Noki's cheeks.

"Noki?"

"I saw Eti sitting on the Son God, Jesus' lap." Noki could not stop his tears. Antonio enveloped the boy in his arms and comforted him while Noki mourned. The boy had kept his feelings bottled up far too long.

When he regained control of himself, Noki pulled away and wiped his eyes on his sleeve.

"Are you feeling better?" Antonio asked.

"Yes."

Noki was chagrined at the dark stains that blotched Father Antonio's habit, but he was grateful for the priest's understanding.

Father Antonio walked around the stone carving. His eyes lit up with sudden inspiration. "Jesus Christ is the fountain of living waters," he exclaimed.

"Fountain?"

"A fountain is water that flows out from the ground, sometimes shooting into the air. In the scriptures, Jesus calls Himself the fountain of living waters and whoso drinketh of His waters, His teachings, shall never thirst."

"May I read about that when you teach me to read?" Noki asked.

The priest's blue eyes showed his pleasure. "Of course you can, Noki. I also want you to be able to read the art books I brought with me."

"Why, Padre?"

"Because you have a great talent and I would like for you to help me make statues for the mission buildings."

"Me?"

"Yes, Noki. What you call seeing into the stones is a talent; a gift of great proportion. It is a gift from God."

Noki could say nothing; he was so surprised. Statues like those in the Mission San Juan Capistrano? Things that everyone would see? He couldn't believe it.

"I would like for you to begin tomorrow," Father Antonio added.

"What?" Noki asked, not believing what he was hearing.

"I would like for you to complete this sculpture of Jesus. When the lavandería is finished, water will flow from the mouth, a representation of the living water of which I spoke," the priest further explained. "You will have to rework the second stone here," Father Antonio pointed. "Chisel it out so that when we make the tiles, we can form several to funnel the water down through the back of your sculpture and out of the front here." He paused, rubbing his chin in thought. "I want everyone who comes down here to fill their water jugs to be reminded of Jesus and how generous He is with His blessings." Father Antonio studied the back of the stones. "If you can, take off some of the stone at the back, too. It will make the statue lighter and we can set the face into a wall of bricks."

Noki was still trying to understand all that had happened to him. He remembered how Maria had told him he would find his path. Maybe now he had.

"I would like you to begin your reading lessons after you have talked to your uncle and aunt. Since you will be working out here, perhaps we can have lessons for an hour after supper," Father Antonio continued.

"Begin reading that soon?" he asked.

The priest nodded.

"Yes, yes, Father, and I will do my best!"

"It will be hard, but I know you can do it."

For a moment it was silent except for the gentle sounds of the stream. Then the bell rang for Mass.

"Let us go and find joy in this new day."

Father Antonio thought he had a gift. Father and Maria had told him the same thing. Noki believed he could soar like an eagle above the clouds. Life was good.

Autumn had come to the area. In the mountains the oaks were dropping their acorns. At the mission, Noki knew it was time to return home to attend his manhood ceremonies. He felt a little apprehensive, having embraced so many of the white man's ways in the past few months.

Juan encouraged him. "Noki, there is nothing wrong with keeping your old life in your heart. It is what made you what you are today. Does it make you any less if you feel the need to talk to Chinigchinich? Your brother is dead, but you remember him and honor him for what he meant to you."

Noki had continued to wrestle with those thoughts over the past month. "You mean if I remember the old gods, the new ones won't send the devil's people to torment me?"

"There were many, many good things in our lives before the Sosabitom came. Should the life we led for hundreds of seasons be forgotten because we enter a new way of life?"

"No. You are right, Juan," Noki said. "But will Father Antonio feel the same way?"

"Have you seen him preventing the races on the night of the new moon, the ones that celebrate Ouiot, the first captain? Perhaps Father Antonio doesn't understand everything about our celebrations, but he understands that certain things from our past help us to be happy with our new lives."

In the end, Noki told the priest he was going to see his parents, which, of course was true.

Father Antonio gave him a blessing. "I will be praying for you and for your father."

Noki was grateful. He missed his father and his mother so very much.

He arrived at the village to find it a beehive of activity. Everyone was preparing to leave for the sacred mountain. He was greeted as though he had been gone a few days rather than the month since his and Father Antonio's last visit. Sachac embraced him. "I have missed you, Noki," she said when she pulled back. She looked him over. "You have grown."

Noki laughed. "Teresa is always giving me extra food. It has not been that long since Father Antonio and I visited."

"I know it hasn't, Noki, it just seems that way. I am glad they feed you well. It will make you strong for the manhood ceremonies. Your uncle finished the arrangements your father began for you to take part."

"I must thank him. Where is he?"

"With Oomaqat in the sweat house."

"And where are Tomás and Gabriella?"

"They are preparing for the journey. You will see them soon."

"I'm going to find Koowut," Noki said. Sachac nodded as she stirred up the fire to prepare lunch.

It didn't take long to find his friend.

Koowut grinned when he saw him. "I heard you were joining us in the manhood rites."

"Of course. It's all I ever wanted since I passed my birth season this year."

"I wondered if you had become so taken with your new Sosabitom gods that you would forget the old ways," Koowut said.

"I have not forgotten the old ways! I have just added good new ways," Noki said testily.

"Your father has no one to follow him in the stone cutting," Koowut pointed out.

"Father is not here."

"I have heard he might return to the village," Koowut said.

"Good!" Noki answered. "If Father comes back, I can make arrowheads when I am here. There is much less need for arrowheads now that people are raising animals and growing crops. I am using what I have learned in other ways now."

Koowut retorted. "I don't know about this business of raising animals and growing white man's food. I hunt! The making of weapons will always be necessary and honorable!"

"My friend, I am not here to argue, but to celebrate. We will soon be men. It is something that will never be taken from us."

Koowut's demeanor softened. "You're right, of course."

Noki's uncle approached. "Are you ready for your ceremonies?"

"Yes!" both boys cried out in unison.

Chaht laughed and clapped them on the shoulders. "Good, we are leaving this afternoon."

"Thank you for arranging my participation in the manhood ceremonies, Uncle Chaht," Noki said as they walked back to his uncle's house.

"I only finished what your father asked me to do," he said. "He sent this to you. He wanted you to wear it when you came." Uncle Chaht handed Noki a small woven grass package.

Noki unwrapped it and stared at the contents. It was Father's knapping tool, the one used for more delicate work, tied to a leather cord. Noki felt tears stinging the corners of his eyes. He knew why Father had sent it. Kwalah was ready to talk to him.

Chaht took the necklace and placed it around Noki's neck. "It is a good day."

Several hours later the villagers left, singing the songs of travel. Father's knapping tool lay against Noki's chest. That night, the old ones told stories of the days when all the animals were people, plotting and playing jokes on each another. Noki curled up in his blanket, content.

The next day they arrived at the sacred mountain. People called out greetings to friends and relatives. He looked for his own family. When he saw them, part of him wanted to run to his mother and father, but he seemed rooted to the ground. Tahmahwit stood by Father's side, Atu in her arms.

Chapter Twenty-six

Noki and his father looked at one another for a moment. Kwalah's eyes traveled down to the necklace around Noki's neck. With a slight movement of his hand, Father motioned Noki to follow him into a nearby house. Inside, Kwalah sat down, regarding Noki who crouched within the entrance. "Sit down, Noki," Father beckoned. "Close to me."

Noki couldn't tell whether his father was angry or sad. He sat down, saying nothing.

"Your uncle told me you were sick while you lived at the white man village. It was the same illness Eti had."

Noki could only nod. His tongue seemed glued to the roof of his mouth.

"I was worried I would lose both sons."

Noki heard a catch in his father's voice.

"Noki, you are my son, I will always love you. Chaht told me you have done well at the mission. Have you decided to stay there?"

"I don't know. I think so," Noki said hesitantly. "I wanted to . . . ask you . . . what you thought if I did...."

"Why? You are a man . . . or will be in a short while. Why do you need to ask me?"

Noki looked into his father's eyes. "Because **you** are my father."

"After Eti died, I thought I had lost two sons. I thought very little of all the times when you brought happiness and pride into my heart," Kwalah said. "But in the past season, I have missed you. Lately I have dreamed of you and Eti. I believe the gods are trying to tell me it is time I welcome you back into our house."

Noki bowed his head. "I'm sorry for the unhappiness I brought you and Mother."

Kwalah leaned over and touched Noki on the knee. "What is done is done. Let us talk with one another as befits a father and son."

Noki reached toward his father and enveloped him in his arms; tears of joy sliding down his cheeks. Kwalah wrapped his arms around his son. Noki felt the wetness of his father's tears on his neck.

Later that night, he and Father sat outside watching the stars. Noki broke the silence. "Father, are you disappointed I'm at the mission working with Father Antonio?"

"Are you happy there?" Kwalah asked.

"Yes, most of the time. I am learning many new skills, and learning things I hope will bring honor to our people."

"I am content."

Noki was dissatisfied with the answer, but didn't say anything.

As though reading his mind, Kwalah continued. "I think the Creator would be pleased you are trying to understand the Sosabitom and get along with them."

"Father, how would you feel if I was baptized?"

"Would that make you happy?" Kwalah asked

Would it, Noki thought? He felt comfortable at the mission now, enjoyed his lessons with Father Antonio. Most of all, he felt useful in what he was doing. "Yes, I think so. I like working with Father Antonio. He is teaching me much. In some ways he is like an uncle to me."

"Perhaps he is teaching you things that will help our people at some future time. But though your hands do something new and different, let your heart always be Payomkawichum."

Noki remembered Kawawish's prophecy to Father Antonio and frowned.

"What is troubling you, son?" Father asked suddenly.

Noki looked up, startled, realizing that it had become very quiet in the little house. "I was remembering something Kawawish told Father Antonio." He told his father about the confrontation.

Kwalah rubbed his chin. "I fear Kawawish may have prophesied truly."

"I won't forget the old ways and when I have children, I will teach them what I have learned from you," Noki promised. "They will know the names of our gods and the language of our people."

"I know you will keep that promise." Kwalah leaned over to stir the coals in the small fire. "Now to more pleasant things. Tell me everything that's happened to you the past several moons."

After talking for some time, Noki spoke of another thing that had been bothering him. "I will still come and make weapons when I can."

"When you can."

"My sons will learn to see into the stones as you do," Noki said with conviction.

"Hopefully they will, if they inherit their father's skills. I will come visit you at the mission and see what you have done. From what you told me, you are very busy."

"Yes, I am." Noki could feel the coolness of the late night air on his back and knew they had talked far into the night. Tahmahwit and Atu had gone into the house several hours earlier.

"Perhaps it would be good for us to get some sleep," Kwalah said. "You will have much less of that during the days to come."

The next morning, the people moved farther into the mountains where the black oaks grew profusely. Directed by a shaman from another tribe, Noki and his friends drank the special drink, the naqtumuc. While under the influence of the drink, he and the others were shown the special dances celebrating their transition into manhood. They danced throughout the afternoon, almost to the point of exhaustion. Later, Noki and the others listened to the advice of the elders on how to conduct themselves as men.

They were led away from the village where they bathed in a nearby stream. Afterward, they were painted by the village leaders. Each color and design had special meaning, reminding them of their duties as men. These instructions and ceremonies went on for several weeks until one morning the elder in charge informed him he was a man.

Noki ran to the village where he presented himself to his parents. Tahmahwit and Kwalah embraced him in congratulation. Atu treated him no differently than she had before. Toddling over, she demanded to be picked up. Tahmahwit fixed him breakfast and later in the day Kwalah took him to the sweathouse. Noki allowed the steam to cleanse his mind as well as his body.

That evening his family's home was filled with the easy banter of familiar, loving relationships. It felt good to Noki after the long separation. There were moments when they sat around the tiny fire without saying anything. Noki knew some of the silence was the absence of Eti. The hollow place in his heart left by his brother's death had been partly filled by his recent activities, but he would always miss Eti.

The next morning, Noki began his trip back to the mission alone, ready to continue his studies and work. A few hours before sunset, he reached the site of the old village. Even though the houses had been dismantled, the sunken foundations of the homes remained. The lowering sun was obscured in clouds and Noki realized there would be rain before the night was over. As he watched, distant flashes of lightning winked on the horizon. With rain coming, Noki decided to sleep in a cave in a nearby canyon.

After building a fire near the entrance of the cave, Noki lay back on his blanket. During his journey, he had caught two quail. They were now roasting over the coals. He went to a stream to wash up before eating. As he rinsed his face and hands, Noki heard a coyote howl. The wind rattled the branches of a scrub tree. They were mournful sounds and he shivered.

The quail cooked to a savory brown, the outer skins crispy. Noki pulled them a bit further from the flames and left them to cool. He pulled out two small ground chia seed cakes Tahmahwit had given him. After taking a few bites, he found he wasn't hungry. He rewrapped them, along with the two cooked birds, and returned them to his pouch.

Noki watched the fire and thought over all that had befallen him in the past six months. It seemed so unbelievable how much his life had changed.

He wrapped himself in his hide blanket and lay near the fire. What seemed to be only a moment later, Noki jerked awake, hearing chanting mingled with the doleful sound of the wind. One song was chanted by a woman; another by a child. Noki crawled to the entrance of the cave. Fog swirled and eddied, making way for ghostly dancers that beckoned to him.

Noki hesitated, afraid of what these ghosts might want. Another appeared with the first and beckoned also. This time Noki obeyed, or rather his feet obeyed. He remembered when he and Eti joked about seeing the Dance of the Dead. It seemed he was going to have that opportunity, and this time the dancers were not disappearing at the sight of the living as they did in the stories.

Noki wondered why he had been singled out for this honor—or was it a curse? *Was this a summons to join them in the realm of the dead?* He shivered again, but something reassured him that it wasn't. For some reason, the wraiths had come to his old village, maybe to see him. Regardless, he could no more disobey them than he could fly to the tops of the trees. Noki followed the two dancers as they continued toward the center of the village. Fog swirled around his feet, rising almost to his knees.

They arrived at the site of the ceremonial house. When he had come into the village several hours ago, the poles, which thrust upward to meet at a center point of the roof, were bare. It had looked like the ribs of a large dead animal, stones piled around it as though one of the gods had thought to bury it. Now the wamkish had been reconstructed, thin branches with tule reeds woven around them in layers tight enough to resist the rain. His two escorts stopped, signing for him to watch. They joined other dancers who were moving in a slow circle around the structure. The wind continued blowing, occasionally lifting a corner of one of the mats but never affecting the fog.

From the inside of the house, two figures appeared, a boy and a woman. They did not crawl through the entrance. It was as though they had been inside and now, suddenly they were outside the doorway.

"Eti!" Noki cried out, recognizing his brother. He started to rush toward him, but Eti raised his hand to stop him. Grinning in a way Noki remembered so well, his brother began a slow dance around him, singing at the same time. His words were clear, with no sign of his speech impediment.

"The Starry Path is a bright one," Eti sang. "It is filled with those who have gone before. It is happy. There is song. We all sing the same song. The god of the Starry Path greeted me and led me. All the gods are singing the same song. Smile, my brother. Sing and rejoice. Hear me and be happy."

Noki couldn't help himself; he grinned with his little brother. Eti was happy. It made his heart glad and his spirit soar. Eti reached out to him, his fingers stopping within inches of Noki's hand.

"Hear me, my brother and feel my love for you." He was now speaking in a normal voice. "See my tears of joy." Small crystal-like tears traced down the ghostly cheek. "Listen to my words, hold them in your heart. Be a friend to Father Antonio. He is a good man. Help him understand our people. He needs you and our people need you."

There was a pause and Noki pondered for a moment all the words his brother told him. "I will, my brother."

"There are sad times ahead for our people. But you can help them through it; you and your children and their children," Eti continued.

Noki looked beyond Eti at the woman who stood there. He realized who it was. "Mother?"

She smiled at him. It was Shehevish, his biological mother. She began to sing as Eti had. The other ghostly dancers moved around them.

"You are a man now, my son. You are my son, with the blood of my father and his father in you. The ancestors rejoice in you. I rejoice in you. Your brother and I watch over you. Be brave. Be strong."

The dancers backed away, becoming more and more ghostly. Eti moved away to join the receding dancers. "Eti!" Noki cried. "Don't go! Please!"

"We must," Eti said, his voice soft like the gauzy strands of the spider's web in the morning.

"We love you," Shehevish said to him. As she walked by him, she reached toward him with her fingers outstretched. Shehevish did not touch him, either, but Noki felt the warm, loving caress like the breath of a warm breeze. He reached out to her, but only felt tendrils of fog as her body disappeared. Eti waved and then he, too, vanished.

The fog coalesced directly in front of him, drawing in from around his ankles, eddying into a column that was about his height. It formed into a figure; a woman. Her hair looked like fog, wispy, but dark. It moved as though the wind was blowing it. Her eyes were deep and fathomless, but they looked on him as a mother's would. This was no woman he had ever met before, and yet she seemed very familiar. She was clothed in a gossamer dress, one that could have been made of thousands of spider webs. Leaves and earth clung to it. In her hands she held twigs of willow and oak, as though she was ready to weave a basket. His gaze kept returning to her face. It was young and old, kind and stern, all at the same time. Her lips curved into a half smile. Noki relaxed.

"Who are you?" he asked. His voice trembled.

"You know me, Noki," she said. "You knew me when you looked into the arrowhead and saw its heart. You knew me when you buried your brother in the earth and when you have prayed."

"Chinigchinich is a man," Noki said and then felt foolish.

The spectral woman laughed. Like her face, he felt the laughter held joy and pain. "Noki," she began.

It dawned on him. "You are Earth Mother," he whispered.

"I am known by many names, and by many people."

Noki didn't know what to do or say in the presence of the holy spirit of Mother Earth.

"Noki, be true to your heart," she said, after several moments of silence. The eyes flashed and the voice rang with conviction. "Your heart is a Payomkawichum heart. Always remember that, even as the Sosabitom swallow the people up. It will be difficult for you and your descendants, but it can be done. I leave you to find your path in the maze of a confusing, changing world."

"Would it be better if I went into the hills where some of the people have gone?" he asked.

The entity shook her head. "There is no place where the people can go to escape what is on the land and in the future. Only in their hearts and souls can the people be true to their heritage and to the spirits who have guided their ancestors." As Eti and Shehevish had disappeared, so too, did Earth Mother. It was like she was drawing the fog close to her body and pulling it with her as she left. Soon there was nothing but darkness; no fog, no entities, no sound except for thunder and the rustling of the wind among nearby trees. The wamkish was once again an empty shell of skeletal poles reaching skyward. Noki felt wetness on his cheeks and realized he had been overcome by the power of his vision. He didn't try to wipe the tears away.

Thunder crashed in his ears and the rain fell. It pelted his body, mingled with the tears that slid down his cheeks. He made his way through the darkness to his cave shelter where he sank exhausted on his blanket. A few drops of rain blew into the entrance, but Noki ignored them. The distant booming beat a cadence in the sky and the wind in the far canyons whistled like a bullroarer.

Noki slept, lulled by the comforting words of his mother and brother.

Chapter Twenty-seven

After he returned from the mountains, Noki finished the stone sculpture for the lavandería, making the adjustments that had been suggested.

Father Antonio taught Noki how to read and write Spanish and Noki helped the priest learn more of his own language and culture. Noki had even begun to learn a little Latin.

"You are very good with languages," the priest told him one cool night. They were in a village in the hills.

"Thank you, Father," Noki said, stifling a yawn. "I like learning and I'm happy to teach you about our people."

"You are a very good teacher, Noki. You would make an excellent priest."

Noki was taken aback. "Me? A priest? Like you?"

"Yes," Father Antonio replied. "Think about it."

"I don't know," Noki said. He knew the priest was giving him great honor, but he remembered his father's words. He remembered Juan's advice. Most of all he remembered the words of Earth Mother. Noki could not teach the Sosabitom ways with the same fervor as Father Antonio, because he didn't feel the white man's traditions were the only way to live. He remembered something else Juan had told him. "Would I have to go far away to learn and teach, Father Antonio?"

"Probably no further than Mexico City. And not more than a year or two."

Two years away from his family? Two years away from the sea and the hills? Two years away from the ancestors and from the sacred earth of this place? "Mexico City is many days journey from here. I don't think I could leave this place. It is my home."

"When you are dedicated to God, it becomes easy to go where He wants you to go," Father Antonio replied. "Perhaps you should take some time to think and pray. You can give me your answer when you are ready."

Noki searched his heart and deep inside, he felt his answer. "Padre, I do not think I need to pray. I already know where my heart is. Please do not feel angry or disappointed with my answer. But my place is here, with my people. The learning you give me is of great worth to me, but I cannot leave the home of my ancestors."

Father Antonio was silent for a moment. In the dim light it was hard to decipher the priest's countenance. "No, Noki, I can't be angry," Father Antonio finally said. "Maybe a little disappointed, because I do feel you would make a great priest. I might have been asking too much of you at such a young age."

"I am learning a great deal from you here, Father Antonio. Why should I go far away to Mexico City?"

Father Antonio chuckled and clapped the young man on the back. "Thank you, Noki. I believe that is the best compliment I have ever received. Now let's review a few of the words you learned yesterday while the fire gives us enough light to write in the dirt. The blessed time of Our Lord and Savior's birth will soon be here and there will be less time for lessons."

"That is the Navidad you have talked about?" Noki asked.

"Yes. There are several Holy Days associated with Jesus' birth, culminating in the special Mass on Christmas Day. After we return to the mission we will spend our time in preparation."

"That is why you have been in the villages inviting all to come to the mission the last two weeks in December."

"Yes," Father Antonio replied. "It will be a very grand celebration."

"Tell me what will happen at these celebrations," Noki asked, feeling the priest's excitement. Celebrating the birth of a god had to be a happy occasion. Father Antonio eagerly complied. Noki thought of Eti's words at the Dance of the Dead. "Father Antonio?"

"Yes, my son."

"Is it permitted for one to be baptized on the Savior's birthday?"

Father Antonio was taken by surprise. "Yes, Noki, it is," he said, his voice soft and filled with emotion.

"That is the day I wish to be baptized."

"Wonderful!"

Noki remembered Earth Mother's words. He would live in the Sosabitom's world, but his heart would continue to be that of a Payomkawichum.

On Christmas Day, after Mass, Noki knelt in front of the stone baptismal font, listening as Father Antonio spoke the Latin words of the Holy Sacrament of Baptism. Nearby were Maria, Tomás and his family. Juan and

Anna, along with all the rest of his friends at the mission had gathered to watch, too. Noki felt the presence of Eti and his mother, Shehevish.

"Chamna, Putunga, Pukaamy, pi Poloov Putoowi," Father Antonio repeated the words in the Payomkawichum language. ("In the name of the Father, the Son and the Holy Spirit.")

"Po'eekup (Amen)," Noki replied, satisfied.

Epilogue

1814

Noki stood quietly with the other men in the choir, gazing at the huge, brilliantly white adobe edifice. The new church was several times the size of the original built fifteen years ago. The little statue of St. Francis looked down at all of them as the men prepared to sing.

He glanced at the women's choir. Maria held their third child, Kwalah, in her arms. He watched the children and was pleased to see Eti, their oldest child, and little Shehevish, their middle child sitting in front of the new church, hands laying in their laps. Their shirts were new, bright white like the walls behind them. Noki frowned as Eti reached down with one finger and began playing in the dust. Then he relaxed. Eti was a child after all, taking after his namesake. All of their children knew about his brother, just as all of them knew about the language and customs of their people.

Father Antonio was clothed in white vestments, embroidered with purple and gold thread. He was showing the effects of the past fifteen years of hard work and dedication, but he was still energetic and traveled as often as he could to the many rancherias in the area.

As Father Antonio raised his arms to begin, Noki took a deep breath. He knew that inside the newly carved doors of the church, stood the embellished font he had finished almost ten years ago.

Noki had worked on many of the more intricate wall designs as well as the statues on each side of the entryway. Father Antonio said this mission would stand for generations. Looking over its brilliant whiteness, its size and grandeur, Noki believed him. He also believed the heart of his people would reside in this church as it did in the land they had trod upon for many more generations than he could count. Future visitors would wonder and feel awe, and hopefully sense his people's spirit residing here. *Looviq*—good, it was very, very good.

Father Antonio began the song, the Te Deum Laudamus. The notes of the celebration song echoed against the new building and throughout the valley.

Noki was content.

178

Susan Kite first visited the Mission San Luis Rey in 2001 with a group of Zorro enthusiasts, (several episodes of the television series were filmed at the mission). She visited two more times, and the story of Antonio Peyri and Noki began taking shape. The author has written extensively over the past decade and a half, but this is her first published work. Ms. Kite is a full time school librarian in Hamilton County, Tennessee. She lives in Athens, Tennessee with her husband, Dan, and several fur-kids.

CPSIA information can be obtained at www.ICGtesting.com
Printed in the USA
237844LV00003B/4/P

9 781609 101602